UNDYING

Other books by Todd Gitlin

NOVELS

Sacrifice

The Murder of Albert Einstein

NONFICTION

The Chosen Peoples: America, Israel, and the Ordeals of Divine Election (with Liel Leibovitz)

The Bulldozer and the Big Tent: Blind Republicans, Lame Democrats, and the Recovery of American Ideals

The Intellectuals and the Flag

Letters to a Young Activist

Media Unlimited: How the Torrent of Images and Sounds Overwhelms Our Lives

The Twilight of Common Dreams: Why America is Wracked by Culture Wars

Watching Television (edited)

The Sixties: Years of Hope, Days of Rage

Inside Prime Time

The Whole World is Watching: Mass Media in the Making and Unmaking of the New Left

Uptown: Poor Whites in Chicago (with Nanci Hollander)

POETRY

Busy Being Born

Campfires of the Resistance: Poetry from the Movement (edited)

Todd Gitlin

Undying

A Novel

COUNTERPOINT
BERKELEY

Library of Congress Cataloging-in-Publication Data is available.

978-1-58243-646-3

Cover design by Silverander Communications
Interior Design by Megan Jones Design

Printed in the United States of America

COUNTERPOINT
1919 Fifth Street
Berkeley, CA 94710

www.counterpointpress.com

Distributed by Publishers Group West

10 9 8 7 6 5 4 3 2 1

One must, from time to time, escape from truth into untruth in order to recuperate, otherwise truth becomes boring, feeble, and tasteless. . . .

—Friedrich Nietzsche, "Against the Tyranny of Truth," *Dawn*

¤ ¤ ¤

For a psychologist there are few questions that are as attractive as that concerning the relation of health and philosophy, and if he should himself become ill, he will bring all of his scientific curiosity into his illness.

—Friedrich Nietzsche, *The Gay Science*

¤ ¤ ¤

Il faut accepter

Pas la mort,
Mais la mienne.

—Eugène Guillevic, "De ma mort"

During the closing weeks of the 2004 presidential campaign, as George W. Bush, in the full flower of rugged health, denounced John Kerry's "policy of weakness" and was consequently hailed by millions of my countrymen and -women as the picture of manly strength, cancerous cells in my lymph glands were breeding at a stupendous rate.

Every element in this sentence is true, but I would never try to convince you that the first set of facts caused the second. There is no reason to believe that my body was more porous than any other body, no evidence, *none*, that my lymphatic system soaked up and amplified the awful disturbances of the outer world and converted a historical pathology into a personal one. I know *perfectly well* that it wasn't the outer calamity of George Bush that brought me inner calamity. I don't take him that personally, and I'm sure he returns the favor. The absurdity of the world does not revolve around the cellular disequilibrium of Alan Meister. Had George W. Bush never existed, or had Al Gore fought smarter and tougher in

2000, or had John Quincy Adams never negotiated the purchase of Florida from Spain, or had Ralph Nader been less stubborn, there's every reason to think that my lymph cells would have gone just as berserk as they, in fact, went.

When you can't feel what you feel, or you're in too deep, you play mind games. I do that for a living.

¤ ¤ ¤

Stuff happens. That nifty little statement by Herr Professor Dr. Rumsfeld about the nature of things might have been the motto for the work that made my name, such as it is—telling humanists and democrats why they should emulate Camus and Emma Goldman and love a philosopher who held humanists and democrats in contempt.

"Freedom's untidy," the sage of the Pentagon continued, four weeks into his gratuitous war.

Every child puts the world to use for his own playful purposes, which have nothing to do with the purposes of others. So every child manufactures untidiness. When I was six or seven years old, we were visiting a family in the suburbs, an almost exotic destination in the eyes of an apartment dweller in those days, a not-quite-settled frontier, and I was playing with the boy of the house, whose name I forget, by the fence in their backyard, poking around in the gravel, and damn if I didn't stick my palm flat onto the point of a rusty nail, which led to (1) an exciting late-night ride to the hospital; (2)

a long sit in the emergency room while the door kept flapping open and letting the snow in, and a man sitting across the room peed his pants while I sat patiently reading the "Most Unforgettable Character I Ever Met" feature in *Reader's Digest*; and (3) an eventual tetanus shot, a dramatic white sling for my arm, and eventually, a scar that runs like a tiny white worm a quarter inch along a lifeline in my left palm. Early the next morning, a Sunday, the phone rang and my probably sleep-deprived parents didn't pick up, so I did. It was my aunt, my father's sister, to say that my grandmother had just dropped dead of a heart attack. What did I do? I rolled over and went back to sleep.

When my father asked me later why I had done that, I apologized and allowed as how I'd behaved strangely and I didn't know why. He was, as usual, reticent. He didn't take his belt to me (that time), for which I was grateful. What I didn't say was that I didn't feel much of anything for the old lady who was, after all, his mother. She smelled stale. She had thin lips, smiled without conviction, and sat like a lump. She wore her limp hair in a net. Later, in college, I realized that the day of the phone call from my aunt was the day I discovered (1) the pleasures of half-truth and (2) the choppiness of the universe. That was the day I was primed to study philosophy.

But let me be generous for a change. My widowed grandmother was, after all, benign. She caused me no harm. It's unfair of me to remember her as an impassive monument—a faintly smiling Buddha. Her placid demeanor might well have been her adaptation to life with her stern and implacable husband, a man who in his youth threw a Cossack down a well during a pogrom, at least according to the family lore. But inertia is what I remember about her, and a man is responsible for his memory in the way Camus said that after a certain age a man is responsible for his face. I realized many years after my father's mother died that my father probably didn't think much of her company, either. He rarely expressed the desire to cross the Whitestone Bridge from the Bronx to Queens to visit her—at least according to my mother (granted, a jaundiced source), who found her not only forbidding but (to be polite) "slow." That was a way of saying "not bright," which was a mark of deficiency in her book and, in fact, in the great book of assumptions kept by the Jews. This grandmother never went to school; she was illiterate as a stone not only in English but in her mother tongue, Yiddish. In any event, it was my mother and not my father who thought that paying two or three visits a year to my father's own side of the family was the right thing to do.

My dutiful mother and her in-law problems. Her father-in-law despised her—on this both my parents could agree. "She has burning eyes," he told my father, who ignored the observation to his later, not infrequently expressed regret. His father didn't mean it as a compliment. Since my mother is more or less blonde, perhaps he saw in her the eyes of the attacking Cossack.

Anyway, it's not that the little injury to my left palm had anything to do with the death of my father's mother. They were sequential, that's all. One pain was survivable, and the other was lethal. One life goes on, another life ends, and in the mind of the one who goes on, the question goes on with it.

It's a great life, as my mother-in-law likes to say, if you don't weaken.

So take heed, astrologers, Marxists, or anyone else who is partial to theories of everything: What takes place outside your skin doesn't necessarily make anything happen inside your skin. And vice versa. Nothing new here. In 1739, Hume blew up the idea that there could be a rational reason to believe that X causes Y. But just because there's no cause-and-effect connecting two events doesn't mean the events lack a connection. It's just that the connection isn't the cause and effect kind—which is the least interesting kind of connection anyway. The easiest to describe, the kind we prefer, but the least interesting. The connection between George Bush and my frantic lymph cells might be the kind where dimensions intersect in some other reality, the way parallel lines meet at infinity. Too bad for us that we don't get to be there when they meet.

But I'm getting ahead of myself. First, surprise and untidiness happened. The ground opened beneath my feet.

¤ ¤ ¤

SPEAKING OF THE strangeness of actions that take place more or less simultaneously and yet are not related as cause and effect—

In the year 1876, one Johann Heinrich Rumsfeld migrated to the United States of America from a town called Weyhe in Saxony. That same year, a thirty-one-year-old professor of philology in Basel, Switzerland, on the German border, took leave from his university post because he suffered, sometimes for weeks on end, from ferocious headaches. He would vomit for hours. He was originally from Saxony, too. In March, this professor, whose name was Friedrich Nietzsche—his friends and family called him Fritz—was at work on a manifesto proclaiming that Richard Wagner's operatic style was the key to rejuvenating all of society. He left Basel, which was about to celebrate its annual carnival—a raucous affair, what with all its fevered drumming, unbearable for a man who suffered from migraine, however highly he valued Basel's version of the drunken rites of Dionysus, which were featured prominently in the book that had brought him a certain renown four years earlier, *The Birth of Tragedy*, dedicated to Wagner, who was esteemed by Fritz for elevating the urgency of art. ("I have concluded an alliance with Wagner," he wrote to a friend then. "You can't believe how close we are now and how our plans coincide.")

So Fritz made his way to Geneva. One reason was that it promised tranquility. Another was that he wished to meet a certain Countess Diodati, who, he had heard, had translated his *Tragedy* book into French. A third was that he wanted to spend time with the conductor of the Geneva Orchestra, who was, like himself, a devotee of Wagner. He did indeed stay with the conductor, whose name was Hugo von Senger. As for the Countess, she had gone insane and was locked up in an asylum. More about Fritz's little adventures with Hugo von Senger later.

¤¤¤

TWO THINGS FELT near-apocalyptic to me in October 2004. One was the seemingly unavoidable victory of the ruinous president in the coming election. The other was a circling fear that I had run out of subjects. I desperately needed a book to write. Without one, I might have to take up a hobby, which I hadn't done since I went off to college and my mother gave my stamp collection away—not that I would have returned to my mediocre albums again, mind you, having lost interest in any pursuit at which I could not excel.

Once upon a time, when I was young and promising, subjects came to me like birds to a feeder. All I had to do was put out the seed. I didn't mind if my rivals in graduate school considered me an intellectual popinjay and later called me JB, for Jukebox, since I could, on demand, divert the young about how Tom's views diverged from Dick's and enlarged on Harry's, and how their thinking evolved and didn't evolve, and where their lapses were, and how they were and weren't revived in the next generation by neo-Tom, neo-Dick, and neo-Harry while Thomasin challenged the master narrative and Ricki and Harriet redescribed it. . . . What did I care as long as I could extract transient melodies from the mental cacophony in my head?

Then I was teetering on the far edge of middle age. The birds moved on. I ran out of concepts. Ideas stopped dancing for me. They stood around like statues, with their arms folded, glaring at each other. So I thought I might see whether I could squeeze some intellectual juice out of new material. I badly needed relief from the awful political facts of early twenty-first-century America. Perhaps I could address my two terrors at the same time, imagining what would be for me a new kind of book.

But of course I would also do what I could to put a stop to the reign of Rumsfeld's boss, the usurper George W. Bush. Kerry campaigners being needed in the swing states, Melanie and I joined a weekend bus foray into the flamingly fall-saturated Pennsylvania hills, to the potentially fertile ground of Scranton. There, Melanie got recruited. The commando in charge of volunteers sized her up, accurately, as a woman who not only lights up a room but enjoys spending time with the people who've been illuminated. Would she move down to Scranton for the rest of the campaign? She would. Since we could afford to forego her editing income for the season, she went off to do the Lord's work for John Kerry: matching people to tasks, distributing lawn signs, training volunteers for the phone bank, putting out fires, whatever it might take to salvage the Republic. For a month, she holed up on a sofa-bed in the home of some local Democrats while I stayed home Mondays through Thursdays, taught, poked around for the new subject to write about, and joined her on weekends.

Saturday mornings, the two of us sat on folding chairs in a union hall basement as little pep talks fired up the weekend militants who swept in by the busload from New York. Maps were distributed, each with certain blocks colored with Magic Markers for reasons it was not given to volunteers to understand. Then we would drive off to find those blocks, get lost, roam around, park, then walk the streets with an eye to minimum conversation (scripted) and maximum leverage (get-out-the-vote flyers). But after a couple of weekends of this sort of dragging around, trying to muster some minimal brio, I was getting to feel overcome, and not by zeal. On Saturday, October 16, by the time we parked on our first designated block, I was overwhelmed by fatigue and had zero desire to leave the car for any purpose whatever. No part of my body wanted to open a single gate or trundle down a single path to knock on a single door to urge a single likely voter to turn out to save the world. So while Melanie did her missionary duty, and mine, I tilted the front passenger seat as far back as it went and slept the sleep of the overcome.

Was it Scranton itself that was depleting me? The sum of too much time on the road and too much fear of defeat?

Awakened by the sound of the door creaking open as Melanie returned to the car, I sorted through these possibilities without conviction. I'm a man who loves my naps. Put me to work for an unbroken hour or two and I will gladly savor the feeling of the valves in my mind shutting down little by little. I will go looking for a mattress—anyone's mattress, anywhere I happen to find myself. In a pinch, I'll seek a patch of floor. I can sleep under a desk. I can sleep in my car on the streets of Scranton. I can sleep in a side room in the Democratic headquarters of Lackawanna County, Pennsylvania. I laughed off my exhaustion. Why shouldn't I feel exhausted? I'm getting old, and I'm carrying George W. Bush on my back.

⌑ ⌑ ⌑

STILL FEELING LACKLUSTER, well on the way down to feeble, I decided to stay in New York for the weekend of October 22. *Feeble*, a word that is almost onomatopoetic: It *sounds* like the crumbling of solid things. Friday night, a few friends were getting together with my friend Mike, to plan a fund-raiser. His baby daughter needed major surgery to fix a congenital flaw in her heart. First, Mike didn't want a child at all. The next thing he knew, his girlfriend was pregnant. The next thing he knew, they had broken up. The next thing he knew, he was the father of a baby girl in need of frequent transfusions until she was old enough for the make-or-break surgery, which entailed a bone marrow transplant, and she became the light of his life, and he was back with the girlfriend and the child he could no longer live without.

Major events in your life take place behind your back. For example, in an apartment near the university, your former graduate student is combing her smoky-black hair and vaguely wondering what might come of an evening date with interesting fling potential, not imagining that this is going to be the game-changer, the night that you and she will always remember as the night she walked into your life and swept you away. The next thing you know, you are that most outlandish man, a happy one who at the same time is no fool. Then, for all you know, on another night, years later, (1) malignant cells by the billions are leaping and bounding toward the nerve receptors of your tender skin, and let's say (2) on a cell phone somewhere in Central Asia a salesman of leftover plutonium from the former Soviet Union arranges to meet a buyer from a jihadist cell.

Or as for (2), maybe not. No evidence has come to light. There may also be (3), at a listening post connected to a relay station far above Central Asia, a sleepy American spy who has been known to wonder why he ever bothered to study Russian staring at this curious phrase *brilliant alloy* that's been tagged by the computer program "Big Ear Brings Good Things to Life" and makes note of the time (3:00 PM) and place (a bicycle shop in an alley behind the former Ministry of Culture) of the projected meeting. History takes place behind your back. I once heard a short-order cook say: "Some you win, some you lose, some you don't even know about."

Darwin revealed that biology takes place behind your back, too, while insisting that human beings, with some effort, can unravel the riddle of their own appearance on earth. Religion agrees that everything important takes place behind your back, and calls this everything "God." But when even your own biography takes place behind your back, and you reject all the religious pseudo-explanations and alibis that (presto-chango!) substitute a word for a theory, where are you?

In humanity's gargantuan self-love and myopia we imagine that we are in charge of our destinies—when if we're lucky we can sand down a few rough edges before we call it a day.

An anti-Nietzschean thought: Perhaps, if we pay close attention, we can feel our ancestors pulling strings behind our backs.

And then it's your child's turn to wonder where you went wrong as *her* parents. For example, your daughter, your first-born, your only-born, the baby girl with the tiny fingers, the one on whom you lavished your patience and intelligence and the touch of your stubbled skin against her always and astoundingly tender cheek, the one who was infatuated with brooms and used to toddle around sweeping the kitchen floor, to no apparent purpose but sheer joy, one day she goes off to college and—something happens—something she cannot understand and you cannot understand and the next thing you know, for reasons she cannot or will not pause to explain, she stops talking to her mother and, after telling you that you're, like, a bad drug and a corrupt excuse for a man, stops talking to you, too.

There was a time when she slept in the closet. When I was a junior professor and Melanie was staving off the moment of truth when she would abandon her dissertation for some more bracing pursuit, we lived in a four-room apartment above a garage. Our landlord, who also ran the garage, was an egg-bald fellow called Bud who, when my graduate-student jalopy broke down anywhere within fifty miles, or maybe even a hundred, would tow it back for a song. People said he had girlfriends strewn here and there throughout the region. But he was helpful in other ways. Once he trapped a possum, stuck it in a trash can, and told me he was going to offer it to one of his "nigger" customers, "'cause they like to eat them." Anyway, the apartment, which was not exactly constructed to code, included a bedroom that featured a square pillar right in the middle. My little girl fancied her room—it was unique, the way a great toy is unique, or one of those "awesome" video games toward which one feels no awe. One morning Melanie got up and went to watch our daughter sleeping and found that she'd climbed out of bed and dragged her blanket into the closet and was fast asleep there. She was eleven.

I'm talking about my daughter who dropped out of college and calls occasionally for no particular purpose, though not, I'm glad to say, to ask for money or to say she's changed her name to Britney.

¤¤¤

BACK TO OCTOBER 22, 2004, when I went to bed in a bland, benign, weary state and woke up in the dead center of night with a sharp pain in my gut as if I'd swallowed a serrated knife.

First I thought the intestinal cramps must have return. A few months earlier, Melanie and I had come back from a trip to India, both of us in a state of gastrointestinal "distress," mine worse than hers, up to and including stupendous bursts of diarrhea the less said about which the better, except that this was the toll you paid for three weeks in a mind-blowingly strange country that your intestines weren't meant for. When you're spending good money to stay in the former prime minister's residence in Jaipur, when your room in this establishment has a twenty-foot ceiling, mosaics, carpets, lavish frescoes of royal figures, a by-the-numbers portrait of the onetime proprietor, and a twenty-five-inch TV, when you dine in a hall every square inch of which, from floor to ceiling and across the ceiling and ceiling to floor, is painted in a red-purple arabesque to shout splendor, when the chandeliers drip down overhead and the pillars are unabashed marble, and you drink plenteously and gorge yourself and think nothing of ordering the chocolate mousse to close the parenthesis, blithely forgetting that you're supposed to stay away from dairy (you're near the end of your trip and you've gotten off pretty much unscathed so far), you're paying the price for your confidence, that is, your innocence, that is, your ignorance. A small price, actually, like the cost of a house call from the only Jaipur doctor listed in *Lonely Planet*. I reached him at eight in the morning, on the golf course, and he promised to come to the hotel. It was a bit jarring that he needed directions, but in any case he did arrive, toting a full case of equipment and smiling with assurances, and let drop that he served as the physician to the local maharaja before jabbing our buttocks with antibiotics.

Later, during the scorched afternoon, in a room above the swimming pool, I was the beneficiary of the best massage of my life, in the course of which the wiry young masseur dripped warm, jasmine-scented oil down my back. He had a knowing look and went about his work as one man to another, with no trace of servility. The diarrhea subsided for a while.

It was reassuring that the doctor wanted to see us again before we flew back to New York. The follow-up visit took place the next day, in his office in a small stucco building on a dusty street. The doctor paused before a small portrait of a holy man, brought his palms together, and bowed his head before examining us, after which he pronounced us fit to fly home.

But the gastrointestinal aftermath lasted long enough in New York that I dragged myself to my doctor, who handed me a bunch of little test tubes with which it ought to be possible to see if I was hosting a parasite. I am of the age to be an obedient patient. I proceeded to perform messy duties with the test tubes, on three successive days, two tubes each time, and took them in to the local lab, only to be informed that I'd used the wrong tubes. I was supposed to use a matched pair, a blue one and a pink one, each time, not any two tubes randomly chosen. "Oh," I reported back to the usually impeccable Dr. Kitagawa, "you didn't tell me that the tubes were color-coded. I thought they were randomly colored and didn't realize the color differences had any significance." All I had left was a single matched pair. Making the most of what was at hand, I spooned my excrement into the proper tubes, took them to the lab, and a few days later learned that I tested negative: I harbored no parasites.

Now, awake and writhing on the wrong side of midnight, gouged out of a deep sleep, I assumed the pain in my gut must be a variant of whatever was wrong with my gut before. Perhaps the single matched pair of test tubes didn't catch the elusive parasite, which by now had six months to flourish. Tapeworms are supposed to be able to grow a hundred feet long.

I went back to sleep, then woke up in pain again. Went back to sleep, woke up in pain, went back to sleep, woke up in pain.

As every teacher knows, some things have to be repeated before they get through.

⌑ ⌑ ⌑

As THIS TORMENT runs deeper than language can take me, I will see what collecting my thoughts can accomplish. The sun rises obliviously. I start this journal.

Then I head downstairs into the radiant sunlight. My body feels like a sack of wet cement. The air is exuberant with the chuck-a-chuck strains of a Santana replica band playing "Evil Ways" down the street to drum up interest in a wishfully named Victory Rally for John Kerry. This should be a little interlude of joy, when the chance of winning hasn't been slammed shut. I lug my body down Broadway, passing a man in dreads at a card table selling a few sad-looking thrillers and self-help books with covers curling from heat and age; hefty Latinas trolling the discount stores for bargains; detachments of white women of indeterminate age, two abreast, pushing strollers; and a hunchbacked old man inching down the sidewalk with his walker. (Will my time come to walk myself down the street with one of those aluminum frames, accompanied by a bored young lady?) My pain is of no interest to any of them. At 106th Street, most of the thin crowd is of Santana vintage, that is to say, my own. I say hello to my old partner-in-radicalism Jerry, who works fervently for the best available Democrat year after year (how does he manage it?), and a few minutes later, as Congressman Charlie Rangel, his voice rasping, suggesting either craftiness or trustworthiness, I'm not sure which, stabs his finger into the light like a man who means victory, I have an urgent and overpowering need to get off my feet. I collapse onto a bench in the sun, where I fail to feel any stronger. A homeless old coot nods out on the curb. I have become one of the old men who hang out on benches in the islands in the middle of Broadway, sopping up sunlight. Time does not enliven me.

Eventually I drag myself home. No one objects that I'm taking up too much space on the sidewalk walking too slowly. New York is tolerant that way—most of the time. (I have been one of the intolerant ones who steps on the backs of the shoes of slowpokes, then apologizes.) The pain comes, goes, returns. The intruder in my gut is growing familiar, like a hijacker who takes hostages during a long trip. I cancel my one weekend appointment. I decide to skip the memorial service for Charlie Prince. Charlie, way back, was a fervent pacifist and Vietnam antiwar leader who won my respect and affection, but he came to sound fatuous and new-agey. Not having seen him in many years, I'd been going back and forth on whether to go pay my respects. The pain decides for me—against. My appetite dwindles. Chocolate almost ceases to console.

⌑ ⌑ ⌑

WHAT I ATE last night: sweet and sour spare ribs, brown rice, a fortune cookie. Insufficiently cooked pork causes trichinosis, a very bad disease caused by a parasite. When I was a kid and we ate Chinese—a rare treat—my father warned against this dread trichinosis, not that I ever heard of anyone coming down with it. I thought he said "chickenosis."

⌑⌑⌑

A PHILOSOPHER'S QUESTIONS to pass the time: Why is there pain? If the nerves evolved in order to transmit warnings, to tell human beings and other animals that something is wrong, that we're endangered and should protect ourselves, why don't we feel tickled, say, instead of pained? Tickling is urgent enough. It gets your attention. Or why didn't some other kind of painless sensation evolve to send a pleasant though still unignorable signal? Next question: Why aren't we also equipped with signals that tell us what's gone wrong, exactly where the problem is located, and therefore what to do? Why don't we have the internal version of warning lights—this one comes on when your brakes are worn, that one comes on when a bulb has burned out, and so on?

Here I go again. How hard it is to relinquish the everyday need to understand causes and how they lead to effects! Why do I feel so rotten? Or to pass the time, let's change the question: What causes a little girl who grew up in a loving household and never complained about it, who skipped around on the sidewalk as if her feet had invented skipping, who hugged and kissed on demand, whose mother took her to ballet lessons every day for years—what causes such a girl, a few fast-forwarded years later, to drop out of college and cut off her parents as if they were dead flowers? Like everyone else, I thrash around in a world of effects—at least we think of the world we inhabit as a world of effects, and so believe that our lives "make sense"—

⌑⌑⌑

But I was talking about the curious association between Nietzsche and the curmudgeonly public servant who informed an unknowing America that there were such things as unknown unknowns. "There are known knowns," said the disturbingly likable secretary of defense, Mr. Rumsfeld, "there are things we know we know. We also know there are known unknowns; that is to say we know there are some things we do not know. But there are also unknown unknowns—the ones we don't know we don't know."

Now, I am mindful that if you dig around in enough underbrush, you will find connections between apparently disconnected phenomena. Cognitive psychologists speak of illusory correlations. Anywhere you look, you can find six degrees of connection. It is the thickness of the mesh of loose connections that guarantees that many things that seem spookily, or let's say extrasensorially, connected, aren't. A has just today thought of calling B, and the same day there arrives in A's inbox an e-mail from B suggesting lunch. This proves exactly nothing. On any given day, A will perhaps have thought of calling C, D, E, and F, too, but doesn't, yet the negative evidence—there's no word from C, D, E, and F in his inbox—doesn't impress him. He clutches at his trophy coincidence. He thinks some remarkable force is at work because a positive association has led him to overweigh its significance. One coincidence crowds out all the failures.

Nietzsche is the virtuoso of the unknowable. The point is not to know but to make the most of a failure to know. His lifelong mission is to bang away—bang! bang!—to spread the word that humanity over and over again has fallen into the same deep trap: the demand for certainty. Certainty comes in many shapes—the Forms of Plato, the God of the Jews or Jesus or Muhammad, the equations of science, the smugness of nations—but it is always the same trap. And no one has set this trap for us; humanity sets it for itself. It's a perverse dare—we construct the precipice, then dare ourselves to have the guts to plunge over it. You have to love Nietzsche for his relentlessness, and laugh—or think of laughing—that it's relentlessness for ambiguity's sake.

But in the spirit of Nietzsche, I don't want to stake out a claim that my story is true. An account does not become worthwhile because it gets its facts right. It becomes worthwhile because it rises to its occasion. It makes a shape for smoke.

"Fascination of the opposing point of view: refusal to be deprived of the stimulus of the enigmatic," he scribbles. Except that you must be as powerful as a whole team of oxen to be energized by the unsolved puzzle, the absent but infuriating God.

¤¤¤

THE STIMULATION I need to distract myself from the all-too-commanding throb in my gut is to while away some time exploring the Nietzsche-Rumsfeld-Saxony connection, to see (at least on the strength of Internet links I can access from home) whether Johann Heinrich Rumsfeld and Friedrich Nietzsche might ever have crossed paths. Wouldn't that be something! But now without much trouble I discover what I should have realized in the first place: The odds are next to nothing, for the Saxony where Nietzsche was born and lived, which then belonged to Prussia and today belongs to the state of Saxony-Anhalt, lies a couple of hundred miles east of Rumsfeld's ancestral Lower Saxony, which is actually in the northwest of the country. So much for the poetry of simultaneity.

¤¤¤

WHEN I TURN to the *Times* for distraction, I see that Bush was in Pennsylvania yesterday, declaring that fighting "al-Qaeda in Mesopotamia," a group that did not exist before he rammed us into war, "is not a diversion from the war on terror. It is the way we will win the war on terror."

I grab a ballpoint pen and scribble over his face.

Melanie and I have been defacing his image since early 2001, and yes, I am fully aware how childish it is to act this way. We transfix ourselves, practicing black magic at the breakfast table to no good effect. There are people so numb or uncitizenly as to go on about their business cluelessly while our stumblebum potentate goes on about his, as if he were not their responsibility. This is not my problem. My problem is the opposite: I am bogged down in a quagmire of rage.

The pleasure this affords is not even masochistic. Nothing distracts from the pain in my abdomen. This is not one of those tender squeezes against the bowel walls, when your nerve endings come alive and surprise you with a brief satisfaction. There might as well be a fist, two fists, inside me, squeezing sensitive organs and letting go only to come back squeezing again.

I look up trichinosis online. The incubation period is one to two days. This isn't trichinosis.

¤ ¤ ¤

If I hadn't been relieved of my gravely inflamed appendix decades ago, I would suspect appendicitis. End of rational thoughts about my condition.

I'm a bundle of throbs, a stream of pain in search of relief.

Today is Saturday, a day of rest for physicians and others whose abdominal regions are tranquil.

I call Dr. Kitagawa's emergency number, make an appointment for Monday. There, I've done *something*.

I call Melanie and mention in passing that I've got a stomachache. She commiserates. I tell her I made a doctor's appointment for Monday. She'll know it's odd of me to make a doctor's appointment for a mere pain in the gut. "Probably India isn't finished with me," I offer. "Tell me about Scranton." She raves about the volunteer turnout. Several walk-ins report that Kerry lawn signs are mysteriously disappearing from their front yards.

The relief I feel hearing her voice trickles away, and I'm left with huge beating waves of pain in my abdomen.

Musing is the philosopher's analgesic: a meager recourse but the only one at hand, and better a recourse at hand than two in the bush.

¤ ¤ ¤

NIETZSCHE'S *WILL TO POWER:* "Essential: Start from the body and use it as a guide." And if the body goes haywire? It will still be the case that "belief in the body is better established than belief in the spirit." I will testify to the body's power. It is "rich," as Nietzsche says. It commands attention. My attention salutes.

¤ ¤ ¤

TODAY WE SHALL not start with the fatuous question *Why is there suffering?* (See above.) One might equally ask, with the proper Yiddish intonation, *Why* not *suffering?* ("You mean, life isn't a fountain?") *Why should I, in particular, suffer?* is an even more useless question, since anyone might ask it, in which case it reduces to the first question. One might just as well pull old Heidegger's chestnut out of the fire: *Why is there something rather than nothing?* (My old teacher Sidney Morgenbesser, with his big toothy grin, liked to say: "If there were nothing you'd still be complaining!") Nietzsche had contempt for these abstract exercises, all the way back to his least favorite pre-Socratic, frigid Parmenides, whom he blamed for rejecting "everything lush, colorful, blossoming, illusory, everything that charms and is alive" in his lust for the crystalline certainty you can only find in abstraction. The next thing humanity knows, Plato is sneering at real, terrestrial life, rattling on in his elegant and hugely influential way that real life amounts to life in a cave, shadowy and derivative. Next, our morose species is pooh-poohing everything earthy, everything palpable, everything aromatic, everything you can see, hear, and touch in favor of a hypothetical Christian afterlife. Nietzsche's great achievement is to cry out, *The hell with heaven! I'm happy as a bear running around this cave! I love the brightly painted colors in the flickering candlelight! I don't mind bumping my head against stone walls! Give me texture over cut-and-dried geometry any day!*

But abstraction is not the only threat to life. Pain also overrides everything lush, colorful, blossoming, etc.

If and when I lose my one and only life, I will have lost everything I was or could have hoped to be, every moment of sweetness, every firing synapse and dumb-bunny epiphany, every syrupy and lascivious thought, every mirthless, envious insult, every spell of stifled rage and sudden potential, every clench of my jaw, every memory whiff (my father forgiving sins of which I was not guilty, my mother breaking out the gift of her lavish smile), every assortment of image, fact, intuition, and error that I've laboriously collected, refined, hoarded, neglected, perfected, and failed to perfect. Whatever project I ever junked will stay junked. Whatever moved me will never move me again, and if a painting, a book, a movie that once moved me moves someone else, it will not move that person in exactly the same way it moved me. I will no longer exist to lose and recover myself, but the world will have lost me. And behind me I will have left—what?

The ho-hum truth of being provisional. Jammed into a sack of sick flesh.

There will be no one here, no one anticipating, no one regretting, no one longing, no one itching, no one scratching, no one thinking, no one trying, no one failing better.

But then, who doesn't already know they're provisional? Even I know. In which case, as a thinker, I am redundant already. So then what else am I good for?

¤ ¤ ¤

NIETZSCHE WASN'T AFRAID of pain. He wasn't afraid of worry, either. The important thing is to live intensely and to know in your bones that you are alive. If pain is the body's alert that you are a natural creature, then bring it on. "Believe me: the secret for harvesting from existence the greatest fruitfulness and greatest enjoyment is to live dangerously." No wonder my enjoyments are weak these days. I live too tamely. I don't mean just that I no longer feel like getting my head cracked by a police club in the service of good works. I don't mean that tenure made me altogether brain-dead. I may simply be played out—it's my seventh decade, after all. I don't mean that I no longer love my wife. I can't even say that I've sunk into domestic stupor. Maybe what I mean is that the biggest adventure I can imagine would be an affair—and for all kinds of reasons I don't *want* to have an affair. Where this leaves me, God only knows.

Nietzsche with his mountainous forehead and cascading mustache did not live so tamely. In his head, he built bombs. "Ah, my friend," he writes in an 1881 letter, "sometimes the idea runs through my head that I lead a highly dangerous life, since I'm one of those machines that can burst apart. The intensity of my feelings makes me shudder and laugh."

As for me, how long has it been since I have lived a day without taking a walk on the splenetic side? I flatter myself that I am serious about self-overcoming. Anyone can rant.

The herd rants in unison. Well, let them paw the ground and grunt—they don't need any help from me.

In 1882, Nietzsche writes: "Build your cities on the slopes of Vesuvius! Send your ships into uncharted seas! Live at war with your peers and yourselves!" Perhaps what Nietzsche means is that while the subterranean fires are raging and the pressure is building up, you can live calmly, in equipoise; that you can carry on, entertaining odd thoughts (serving them salted nuts, putting them at their ease); and that the war against inanity is a joyous (and endless) campaign of civil disobedience.

¤¤¤

MELANIE, MELANIE, PLEASE comfort me.

People always ask how we met. She was a graduate student in English who sought out my Nietzsche seminar on the contrarian principle that if all the feminists said that Nietzsche was a hopeless pig and therefore not worth reading, he might be interesting. At the time, she was in hot scholarly pursuit of Mary Shelley, a woman who was the opposite of weak. Melanie found rather more diversion than she was bargaining for.

She stood tall and erect. Her eyes were large and dark. Her voice was dark, well defined. Her dark hair rested comfortably on her shoulders. The sight of her was galvanic.

She was interested in monsters and doubles—she had just latched on to the subject of *Frankenstein* for her dissertation—and she had heard I was interesting, too. During the first class, she started asking questions about *Crime and Punishment*, which she had read more than once. She wrote a smashing paper about Nietzsche's view of Dostoyevsky, who, he wrote, "happened to me" when he came across a French translation of *Notes from Underground* in a bookstore, casually flipped it open, and had "the sudden awareness that one has met with a brother." Nietzsche's actual brother died before his second birthday, when Friedrich was five.

In the next class, Melanie wondered out loud what Nietzsche thought of Mary Shelley, who had become famous across Europe when *Frankenstein* was published. I said I could not imagine him thinking that *Frankenstein* held a candle to *Tristan und Isolde*, say, or, to confine himself to the English, the incomparable Shakespeare. I could imagine him thinking that if you wanted a great ghost story, you should consider *Hamlet.* The truth was, I hadn't the slightest idea what Nietzsche thought of Mary Shelley except that he wasn't impressed by female writers in the first place. I said he might well have thought, as many of the Shelleys' contemporaries did when the first edition of *Frankenstein* was published anonymously, in 1818, that her husband Percy was the actual author.

That night, thinking I might impress this striking woman, I ventured rather far afield into Nietzsche's Geneva adventure, which had never interested me much before. The standard biographies told me that the Wagnerian acolyte Hugo von Senger took Fritz to meet a slender, blonde, green-eyed, twenty-three-year-old piano student who worshipped him and was staying at an inn along with her younger sister, the two of them having moved to Geneva to study with him. "This is my friend, Friedrich Nietzsche," von Senger said. "Be honored, dear girls, that he has come to see you." Von Senger understood that the unworldly Fritz had only the most limited experience of women, and thought that he might fancy the younger sister, but Fritz was taken by the older one, whose name was Mathilde Trampedach, and who was said to resemble the impossibly delicate women painted by Fra Filippo Lippi.

Perhaps stimulated by von Senger's knowledge that Byron had once lived in a nearby villa, the two men sat in the sunlight and talked about poetry. Mathilde could not see Fritz very well, since he was shielding his weak eyes with a heavy green parasol. But she found him "a most exquisite personality." She was sufficiently dazzled by the two men's conversation that she was moved to recite a German translation of Longfellow's tribute to willpower, "Excelsior," perhaps because they were at the edge of the Alps and the poem concerns a young Alpine mountain climber whom the villagers repeatedly warn away from a forbidding mountain pass menaced by ice, snow, and avalanches; and perhaps also because she found the famous Nietzsche melancholy and yet somehow alluring, and because he mentioned that he enjoyed strolling in the mountains, and because the young man in the poem has a sad brow and bears "a banner with the strange device/Excelsior!" and is still clutching it when he is found "half-buried in the snow" at twilight, whereupon out of the cosmos falls a voice resounding with one word: *Excelsior!*

Nietzsche had never heard of this Longfellow before, but was interested to make his acquaintance, for he believed Americans to be particularly herdlike; the only one who had previously interested him was Emerson, with his wild paeans to self-reliance. The lovely Mathilde offered to write out the German translation of "Excelsior" for him.

A few days later, von Senger invited the sisters to accompany the two men on a carriage ride along the shore of Lake Geneva to the Villa Diodati, the family home of Nietzsche's mad translator—and the same house where, it turned out, Byron had summered in 1816. The April weather was lovely. The talk turned to romantic poetry, and then to human freedom. The two men were immersed, but Mathilde grew bold. She couldn't contain herself, she wrote later, from saying that it amazed her that when men got excited by the thought of Byronic revolts against tyrants, they hardly realized how self-conscious and inhibited they were—how *inwardly* stifled. Their outer bondage, she thought, was less burdensome than their inner bondage. Nietzsche stared deeply at her, dumbfounded.

There was one more meeting. Fritz returned to Mathilde's inn to say farewell. Suddenly he went to the piano and launched into a stormy crescendo of thundering chords that eventually subsided into ethereal harmonies that Mathilde experienced as a sort of friendship hymn. Then he rose, started to speak, and thought better of it. He bowed deeply and parted.

Fritz went back to von Senger, who was something of an expert on marriage, having been married twice, and asked his advice. Von Senger withheld the fact that he had his eyes on Mathilde himself—so much so that he had already determined to make her his third wife. The eager Fritz knew nothing of this, nor did he realize how taken she was by the dashing von Senger, not least because he had such an imposing friend as Nietzsche. Von Senger suggested that Fritz write to her. While Fritz wrote, von Senger visited Mathilde with an urgent message. The following morning, he said, she would receive a detailed letter from Nietzsche. She should read it calmly and answer only after mature reflection.

Perhaps Fritz was now thinking about what Wagner had told him: that his ailments were caused by his unmarried state. Wagner might have meant that he suspected that Fritz was innocent of sex, except perhaps the occasional episode for hire. He might have known that Fritz suffered from syphilis, which he might have contracted after an encounter with a prostitute. More unknowns. In any event, Fritz's letter to Mathilde came right to the point:

> Gather all the strength that is in your heart so that you will not be frightened by the question I now put

> to you: Will you be my wife? I love you, and I feel as though you were already mine. Not a word about how quickly I've fallen! . . . Don't you share my faith that together each of us could become freer and better than we could separately, and so "excelsior"? Will you dare to come with me, a man who strives with all his heart to become better and more free? On all the paths of life and thought? . . . Triumph over yourself! Decide quickly! Send me a yes or a no by 10 tomorrow morning!

Oh, in 1876, a love letter was a *love* letter. . . . Still, what Mathilde sent him was a no, though unfortunately, her reply no longer exists. We do have Nietzsche's reply to her: "You are so magnanimous as to forgive me, I feel it in the mild tone of your letter, which I certainly do not deserve. I have suffered so much over my cruel and violent behavior that I cannot thank you enough for your gentleness. . . . My parting wish is that if you should sometime read my name or see me again, you will not think only of the horrors that I have inflicted upon you."

¤ ¤ ¤

BUT I WAS talking about Melanie, whose eyes were alluringly dark, and how hard I tried to impress her (though not by pounding on the piano). So what, she wanted to know, did this quaint tale have to do with Mary Shelley? Just this, I said. The summer that Byron spent at the Villa Diodati, a young poetical guest rented the lakeshore cottage next door. This was Percy Shelley, who had run off from Mrs. Shelley with his lover, Mary Wollstonecraft Godwin. It was a freakishly stormy summer, probably because of a gigantic volcanic eruption in Indonesia the previous year. Byron and his companions had to spend much of their time indoors. One particularly fierce night, they all dined together (with other friends of Byron's) and stayed overnight at the villa. For diversion, they read ghost stories to one another. They decided to hold a contest and write their own. The story Mary started to make up that night was *Frankenstein*. The next day, she started writing it.

When I got to the punch line, Melanie said, "Wow. And by the end of the year, Shelley's first wife, to whom he was still married, had drowned herself. There was more than one reason why the Gothic imagination flourished then."

My dark lady. I could scarcely wait till the end of the semester to ask her out.

¤ ¤ ¤

ON OUR FIRST date, she asked me whatever happened to Nietzsche's beloved Mathilde Trampedach. Before our second date, I checked. She went on to become the third wife of Hugo von Senger. They had two children. One was

Alexander, a minor Nazi architect who published an article called "Race and Architecture" in 1935. The other, Maria, a pianist, anglicized her name to Mary and Frenchified her last name to "de Senger." Evidently she was reluctant to identify as German, a reluctance that Nietzsche would have well understood, having at various times been so eager to cut his ties to the Germans that he fancied himself Polish.

⌑ ⌑ ⌑

MELANIE, MY TRUE and only wife, will care for me—will try to, at least, which is enough. Would I care as much if I were in her place? If I heard in her voice the same gravity she heard in mine, I would be hers, absolutely. I would submit like one of those robed, whirling Sufis incandescent with the gift of their surrender, holding one palm upward to greet the emanations of God and permit them entry into the body. Yes, I would do just as she does. Martyrdom has acquired a bad name and Nietzsche scorns it (for good reason) but I would like to think—I do think—that with a martyr's intense delight I would change places with her.

Whether I would care for her as well as she will care for me is another question. Of course I might find the residual Calvinist in charge. She might caress me, grant me a day flat on my back, and then, the next day, tell me to suck it up and get on with my life. The inner ascetic might be right; who knows?

If I don't deserve this pain, she doesn't either.

Earnest, lugubrious Alan! This moaning is premature and unhelpful. Whatever has hijacked my will has also hijacked hers—as if there could be a hijacking without a hijacker. Since there cannot be, what shall we call what is about to happen to her?

The ordeal of love.

⌑⌑⌑

I SLEEP. IN the middle of the night I bite my fist to stop the pain.

⌑⌑⌑

IN *JOYFUL KNOWLEDGE*—a better translation than the famous but old-fashioned version, *The Gay Science*—Nietzsche brings some good news and betrays his profound *envy* of women:

> we have to give birth to our thoughts out of our pain and, like mothers, endow them with all we have of blood, heart, fire, pleasure, passion, agony, conscience, fate, and catastrophe. . . . And as for sickness: are we not almost tempted to ask whether we could get along without it? Only great pain is the ultimate liberator of the spirit.

Does he mean that we should enjoy pain? No. But does he mean that we should make it pass in a hurry? Not at all:

> Only great pain, the long, slow pain that takes its time—on which we are burned, as it were, with green wood—compels us philosophers to descend into our ultimate depths and to put aside all trust, everything good-natured, everything that would interpose a veil, everything that is mild, that is medium—things in which formerly we may have found our humanity. I doubt that such pain makes us "better"—; but I know that it makes us more profound. . . . one emerges as a different person, with a few more question marks—above all with the will henceforth to question further, more deeply, severely, harshly, evilly, and quietly than one had questioned heretofore. The trust in life is gone: life itself has become a problem—Yet one should not jump to the conclusion that this necessarily makes one gloomy! Even love of life is still possible—only one loves differently.

¤ ¤ ¤

One loves differently. . . . ask me what that's like when the pain passes, please.

And then again, not so fast! On the other hand—and Nietzsche is a man of at least two hands, one of which is always in your pocket if he isn't tickling you—on the other hand, later in the same book, he writes:

> In pain there is as much wisdom as in pleasure: like the latter it is one of the best self-preservatives of a species. Were it not so, pain would long ago have been done away with.

He thinks that whatever lasts must have survival value. Not only does he declare the death of God, but he is a resolute Darwinian, if an unsophisticated one. No wonder the Christian zealots loathe him. They would do so more vocally if they could pronounce his name. But to continue:

> We must also know how to live with reduced energy: as soon as pain gives its precautionary signal, it is time to reduce the speed—some great danger, some storm, is approaching.

So one must live dangerously, but dance away from the danger. . . . Nietzsche's raga, the exultant, twisting style of his thought.

If this isn't enough, just a few lines down he extends his third hand and proceeds to write about men who, when severe pain comes to them, rejoice—they feel summoned to "their supreme moments! These are the heroic men, the great pain-bringers of mankind." You want to appreciate these "rare ones" who despise smug comfort—but you don't want to be them.

And who am I? One of the little men whimpering for comfort. Pathetic.

¤ ¤ ¤

WHEN MELANIE SUFFERED from morning sickness, she didn't whimper. When the nausea subsided, she kept reading *War and Peace*, whence Natasha's name, of course. Somewhere along the way, she gave up on Mary Shelley, monsters, and doubles, and decided that she'd be happier as a freelance book editor for hire than as one of those academics who's always forcing the subject, trying to bend the conversation back to her specialty. When she went into labor, she didn't whimper either.

Don't lecture women about long, slow pain, even if you're the author of *The Birth of Tragedy*.

In any event, Melanie has plenty of good reasons to believe in detours. Detours, diapers, dramas, and dioramas. When Natasha was in diapers but not yet toddling around looking for sharp objects to stick in her mouth, Melanie decided to try her hand at a screenplay, the approved art form for the attention-deficient. Resourceful girl—she figured she could scribble a few lines here, a few lines there, at nap time or even during those absorbing moments when her breast was otherwise occupied. "It's either screenplays or aphorisms," she said, "and I can't do aphorisms. Now that I have no choice, I'm going to become who I am."

"Nietzsche probably turned to aphorisms because he suffered from horrible headaches," was my non sequitur. "The connections between the thoughts escape my memory," he wrote to a friend during his crisis year of 1879. "I have to steal the minutes and quarter-hours of 'brain-energy,' as you call it, steal them away from a suffering brain." Stealing the minutes—on this score if no other, he might have qualified as a parent.

"That's awfully reductive of you," said Melanie.

"You're right, and touché," I said.

Is this my art form? The stutter-start journal, the self-interrupting rant? The torn veil of tears?

¤ ¤ ¤

Monday, October 25

Dr. Robert Kitagawa, my elf of an internist, palpates my abdomen and asks how long I've been aware of the bulge that rises beneath my breastbone and runs down the left side of my distended belly.

During two days of pain it did not once occur to me to probe around my abdominal area. Less than a month ago, the good doctor gave me a routine physical. There was nothing unusual about my abdomen then. Now, the skin of my belly is pulled taut around something firm and huge, akin to a beach ball. How could I miss such a thing? Melanie is always saying that I don't live on the planet Earth, and now I've proved it again. Not that I live somewhere better, just different.

My mind is adrift from my body. My words float out of my mind as if of their own volition: "What could it be?"

"There's not supposed to be any organ there," he says with his usual shading of information and curiosity flecked with irony. "Could be your spleen or your liver." He hesitates. "But that's not very likely." I wait. "Could be lymphoma or leukemia," he says casually, ludicrously.

"Lymphoma," I repeat. My mother came down with non-Hodgkin's lymphoma at eighty-three and a half, three years ago. Underwent chemo, lost her hair, regained her hair, came back, and now seems as well as an eighty-seven-year-old feels. Which is to say, slower than an eighty-three-year-old, but there are many reasons why that might be.

"Hmm," says Dr. Kitagawa. "It's not usually genetic."

Usually, that medical weasel-word. You could drive a truck through *usually*.

"Could it be more of whatever I picked up in India?"

He pauses and then says, "Could be," with a little smile of concession. He sets up a CT scan for me late the next day. "CAT scan," it's pronounced, which makes it sound warm and furry. I have a vague idea that this is like an X-ray but more so.

¤ ¤ ¤

It's a sign that something huge is happening that the mind automatically lapses into cliché: "This can't be happening."

"Ah, but it is," says the spider to the fly.

"But I was just flying along, minding my business," says the fly.

"So you were," says the spider. "Isn't that interesting?"

¤¤¤

I call Melanie's cell phone and get her voice mail, then call the Kerry office in Scranton. When she picks up, after one ring, I try to sound dignified, but she knows.

"What's wrong?"

I relay the news from Dr. Kitagawa.

She skips a beat. It is probably her heart skipping a beat. Hearts do that.

I tell her about the CAT scan appointment.

She doesn't hesitate. "I'll be there."

"Don't drive tonight."

"You sure you're OK?"

"I'm OK. I mean, I feel like I probably sound, but I'll be OK."

"I'll leave at the crack of dawn."

"Thank you."

"*Thank* me? Don't be ridiculous, goofy man."

"I need you," I say gratuitously.

"I'll be there."

When she speaks these words, instantly I feel lighter.

But not for long. After we hang up, the tide of pain slams back into place, the place it has carved out for itself inside me, flooding into every nook and cranny known to me and some not known. The pain comes in swells, in surges, until I, who was once the solid shore, am only this oceanic pain. My mind is a minor appendage, an outer planet, whining: *I don't deserve this.*

⌑ ⌑ ⌑

MOMENTS WHEN ARTICULATENESS fails are moments worth sharp attention. This is the discovery of modern poets, for whom I am the ideal reader. When a brilliant writer lacks for words, I am peculiarly moved, for it is a sign of a hilarious possibility: that the whole enterprise of human intelligence is destined to run aground.

⌑ ⌑ ⌑

NATASHA, DURING HER first year away at college, used to write home complaining that her professors professed not to know the answers to elementary questions. They seemed proud of their ignorance. I tried to convince her that this was a time-honored pedagogical device, a Socratic pose, and that it was a marker of wisdom, even if Socrates himself was putting his interlocutors on. She thought it was childish.

Do teachers have any idea what spells we cast for better or worse? We believe it's our mission to disconcert those who have never before been required to think, but do we realize how we may freak out the unready, or how our offhand remarks go down in the memories of others as luminous aphorisms?

One of the Nietzsche sources I have been consulting is a collection of his letters edited and translated by Peter Fuss and Henry Shapiro. The translations are admirably plain, less stiff and formal than others. As it happens, Peter Fuss was my freshman-year section man in philosophy—a graduate student who gave you a chance to approach the mysteries in a classroom of twenty-five rather than a lecture hall of seven hundred. He was curly-haired, with a high forehead, eyes set close together. He seemed approachable enough—young enough too—that I traipsed over to his office, late in the spring semester, to ask his help in my perplexity. I think this was the first time I ever approached a teacher outside class. I was seventeen.

"When I read Nietzsche," I said, "I think he is brilliant and convincing. Then I read A. J. Ayer, and I think *he* is brilliant and convincing. Then I read Camus, and I think he's right. Now, they can't all be right."

He heard me out and replied: "You pays your money and you takes your choice."

I thought this was profound. I still do. I departed in an exalted state. Perhaps I am still in it, paying my money, taking my choice.

Consider my grandfather Leib, on my mother's side, who set out to raise a family in the United States, and that's what he did. But for a mild man, his life was determined by surprises—two of them. First, having emigrated from Russia to New York, he expatriated himself a second time and went off to fight in the Jewish Legion of the British army in Palestine, against the Turks, for the liberation of the Holy Land. A portrait of Chaim Weizmann hung on his wall all the rest of his life. Back in New York, when his cousin, a married man with a four-year-old daughter, contracted stomach cancer and died, in his twenties, he stepped up and did the approved thing: He married the widow. They had three more children. All four of them loved the man, which is an easy thing to do in Yiddish. They called him Poppa. He was kind and reliable. He didn't laugh very often, and when he did, it was almost soundless. He ran a tiny fruit and vegetable store in the Bronx. It was deeper than it was wide. At four every morning, he left home and took the subway to the Hunts Point market to pick out the highest-quality produce. At one point he gave up his fourteen- or sixteen-hour working days, bought an apartment building, rented out two apartments, and lived in the third—only to lose the whole thing, smash, in the Depression. He picked himself up and started another store. He never owned anything again. He marked prices with a yellow pencil stub on cardboard taken from ironed shirts. When the weather was warm enough, he sat out front on an upended orange crate. He coped with his wife's resentment and temper—she never finished school, but knew she was smart and cut out for higher things. His modesty was defensive. Comfort was not his objective, nor wealth, nor, in fact, happiness. Lesser contentment would do. He was rescued by low expectations.

My mother may have learned from him that duty preceded love. Therefore she married my father.

Whereas I set out to understand the impossibility of squaring circles, i.e., to become a mathematician—from which philosophy was my first detour. Philosophy in the United States meant analytic philosophy, the slicing and dicing of problems until nothing remained of them but specks. This approach dissolved the desire to square circles at all. I started down that road at the beginning of my graduate school years—from which Nietzsche was my second detour, a grand one, and not a minute too soon. I also set out not to have children—from which Natasha was a third detour. And now—

My new motto is: Enjoy your detours.

⌑ ⌑ ⌑

A STORY OF pain is still a story; it can be set in order even if the middle sags and the end doesn't quite arrive. Breathe in, clench teeth, shout, curse, relax, wait for renewed pain. Even a scream has a history, modulations, a beginning, a middle, an end. Someday even my beloved—my wife, or widow, as she may well be soon, recovering from a screwy but I believe rewarding life shared with yours truly—even my beloved will wonder at the strangeness of the story of the blob, my monster, my double.

And my errant daughter, whatever detour she may find herself absorbed in, whoever she is becoming, will she come to regret that she walked out of my life and shows no sign of wanting to walk back in?

¤ ¤ ¤

I WOULDN'T BE telling the whole truth if I said that I always saw a signpost that screamed DETOUR each time I detoured. I never lost the impression that I was actually on the right road—in fact, that I'd never left it. Beautiful complacency, the health of the lazy!

¤ ¤ ¤

DO MY EYES amaze me? Is this vague shape heaving into view . . . at last . . . could it be . . . *a new subject*? Even, mirabile dictu, an idea? Yes! I begin to feel that I am laboring like an ant, hauling a crumb, steady and unfazed, inching my way uphill toward some intuition that can be spoken of without embarrassment as an idea. I catch wind of the aroma of an idea. I can taste it. I know how good it would be to have one. Even if it isn't exactly a new idea. An actual, walking, talking, full-bodied idea may strike you once per career, if you're lucky—most likely in your twenties. And then you busy yourself keeping track of what the significant precursors (and a whole lot of semi-significant or even deservedly forgotten ones) had to say about it. Well, the point of intellectual life, after all, is not originality, which is only a synonym for faulty memory, as Mark Twain is supposed to have said—an aphorism of which Nietzsche certainly would have approved. (He liked Twain. One of his correspondents noted that Nietzsche read aloud from a book of Twain's humorous stories. Who said Nietzsche had no sense of humor?) The point is to put your will to power to work for you, to travel to what Nietzsche called "a country of my own, a soil of my own, an entire discrete, thriving, flourishing world."

For years, I've been disgruntled with my ancient work on Nietzsche's longing for God, the theme of my dissertation and the expanded book that once upon a time got me tenure: *Archangel of the Will.* It wasn't wrong to have argued that Nietzsche longed for God. I still think that he replaced one God with another, leaving behind his beloved Dionysus, who was only the most exuberant God among many, in favor of Zarathustra, a winner-takes-all monodivinity who willed everything that exists. But I outgrew my original interest in Nietzsche's wrestling matches with God. *Archangel* was the book of a man in his late twenties—let's face it, a man who (like Nietzsche at that age) hadn't lived much and was years away from grasping the reality that when he would tell his daughter to keep the caps on her Magic Markers as she crawled up on his desk and chair and leaned over the manuscript on his desk, she wouldn't comply.

Now, in pain, "long, slow pain"—"burned, as it were, with green wood," as dear Fritz would say—the new theme comes to me: Nietzsche's thought as the thought of a sick man, a militantly sick man, a man therefore militantly hostile to the bourgeois type who basks in smugness about his health, the type who when you ask him how he is, shoots right back, "Really well," or "Really, really well." Does a man living a full life need to impress you? *Health* is the complacent man's term for his inertia. The "robust health" of the jogger, the tanned look of the golfer—these would have met with Nietzsche's overflowing contempt. It's against the spiritually flabby comfort-seekers that he casts himself as the patient (in both senses). By contrast, he sees himself as "a man who desires nothing more than to shed daily some comforting belief."

As I say, it's not that I willed the pain in my gut. But pain struck me as one hell of a subject—though not a new one. In brute fact, it's no secret that the Saxon knight-errant of vitality is a professional convalescent who is laid up day after day, month after month, year after year, starting at age twelve, by blinding, exhausting migraines, with "extremely persistent and agonizing pain in the head" and attacks of uncontrollable nausea. After one crisis, he writes to his doctor:

> My existence is a *dreadful burden*: I would have rejected it long ago, had I not been making the most

> instructive experiments in the intellectual and moral domain in just this condition of suffering and almost complete renunciation—this joyous mood, avid for knowledge, raised me to heights where I triumphed over every torture and all despair. On the whole, I am happier now than I have ever been in my life. And yet, continual pain; for many hours of the day, a sensation closely akin to seasickness, a semi-paralysis that makes it difficult to speak, alternating with furious attacks (the last one made me vomit for three days and three nights, I longed for death!). I can't read, rarely write, visit no one, can't listen to music! I keep to myself and take walks in the rarified air, a diet of eggs and milk. No pain-relieving remedies work. The cold is harmful to me. . . . I have already lost consciousness several times.

"For several interminable years it got worse," he writes on another occasion, "reaching a peak of constantly recurring pain at which I had two hundred days of suffering a year." More than half the year! The Wunderkind who would "believe only in a God who knows how to dance" spends his working life—the years before he goes stark raving mad—shouldering the burden of being his brave, afflicted self, scribbling in dimly lit rented rooms on top of one insufficiently magical mountain after another, scratching away on paper about the need to overcome himself, to break out of the prison house of his past and, in fact, humanity's whole prison compound where people willingly reject life for wisps of heavenly fantasy. When turns in the weather afflict him (too hot, too bright, too cold, too damp), he heaves himself back on the road in search of a more favorable stopping-off point. This chronically sick man is obsessed with health and healthy-mindedness. He who exalts the beast of prey is himself prey in waiting. A man who can hardly see, so ferocious are his headaches and eye aches, sneers that the resentful soul "squints."

⌑ ⌑ ⌑

I'VE ALREADY LIVED years longer than Nietzsche did—not to mention Jesus—so what did I expect?

⌑ ⌑ ⌑

MY PARENTS WERE barely sick a day in their lives until they were well into the eighth or ninth decade. Idiocy of the idea of progress.

⌑ ⌑ ⌑

I'M ALSO SANER than Nietzsche was for his last ten years. What does that get me?

⌑ ⌑ ⌑

October 26

It's barely ten o'clock when Melanie walks in. The whites of her eyes are red but her pupils are bright with care, and I'm speechless until, my arms around her, I say stupidly, "Thank you."

"Did you ever think for a split second I wouldn't come? If you were in my position—?"

"This is going to be hell for you."

"In sickness or in health, remember?"

"Right. Right."

We're stammering, as if on a first date.

¤ ¤ ¤

In the waiting room of Union Square Diagnostic Imaging, at the end of normal working hours, I sip a banana-flavored elixir of barium ("contrast solution") with a metallic taste, a chemical concoction resembling no substance that ever sprang from the soil of God's green earth. It's more like the plastic food doled out to passengers en route to the moon in *2001: A Space Odyssey* by the Stepford-smiley stewardess who minces down the aisle in robe and Velcro slippers. That's one of the best things in the film, the eerie punctilio with which the blank-faced troubleshooter with the empty name Heywood Floyd inspects the various primary-color liquids arrayed on his plastic tray, each in its cute little cup, before making his choice.

Come this way, undress, put on this robe, please, you may wear your socks and shoes, this won't take long, you may taste a metallic taste in your mouth, that's normal—and you're ready to be rolled like a hunk of meat into the thick torus of a CT-scan machine in an air-cooled chamber. The metallic taste appears, on cue. The cold, smooth, creamy plastic surface is an inch from my face. A metallic voice, commanding, stentorian: *Breathe in. Hold your breath. . . . Breathe.* This is for my own good, my own good, my own, good.

You may dress now.

Back into the waiting room to find that everyone but Melanie and a stranger has left. The stranger is a man younger than I, sporting a tiny brush of a mustache. He says, "If Bush wins, we'll all be living inside life-support machines." I nod. "I used to be a Republican," he adds. We are weirdly jovial, my fellow passenger and I.

¤ ¤ ¤

October 27

Dr. Kitagawa calls in the morning, practiced and clear, getting right to the point. I'm in my office pretending to work.

"I have the results from your CAT scan. There's a mass, and it's large."

"What is it?"

"Your lymph glands."

"Lymph glands."

"It's not your liver, not your spleen, none of your organs. Your lymph."

At such moments you seek to rescue yourself by tossing distractions around.

"Any chance it's an infection left over from India?"

A telltale, terrible pause.

"It's possible. Not very likely."

"How serious is this?"

"It's pretty serious."

He gives me a list of specialists.

All that comes to mind is:

"Well, thanks."

⌑ ⌑ ⌑

I CALL MY old high school friend Barry, now a hematological oncologist. We talk politics for half an hour. But he knows why I'm calling him for the first time in fifteen years.

He's encouraging. Lymphoma is "treatable and curable." Treatments have advanced by leaps and bounds in recent years. His wife had lymphoma herself, was free of cancer for ten years, is now being treated (with chemotherapy) for a metastasis. He will send me a manual he wrote to explain everything to patients.

There is an unholy trinity with which we treat cancer: cut, burn, and poison. Chemotherapy is the poison part.

Treatable = can be cut, burned, and poisoned.

Curable = can be cured, does not = guaranteed to be cured.

Guarantees are null and void.

Having cancer. Being had by cancer. Conscripted.

¤¤¤

FIRST, CONSCRIPTION. THEN, basic training. It starts with the insult of having been chosen. Not only have I been plucked out of my life and plunked down in another country, I am required to pay my own ransom. There are brand-new rules and procedures. Dexterity and persistence are mandatory. It's like graduate school: Take one course at a time. Take this one before that one. Line up your committees. Pause to size up the situation. Be mindful of the tried-and-true. Be scrupulous. Don't coast. Stay alert. Never relent.

By the way, hurry. Inertia is not on your side.

I start calling the A-list of specialists that Dr. Kitagawa recommended. They're booked for weeks or months ahead.

But first things first. Whatever specialist I end up with to treat me, I first have to be seen by a diagnostician. Diagnosticians are a distinct category of docs. The first appointment I can get with a diagnostician is November 1, the day before the election.

¤¤¤

LIKE AN INFANT with cramps, like a captive buried alive, like a herd of speared elephants, I want to *roar*.

No, I want to dive out of the window, take some smug son of a bitch in a stretch limo with me.

No, I want to leave my dead skin on the ground and wriggle away.

No, I want to laugh till I ache—laugh, I thought I'd die—and then laugh till I no longer ache and not stop laughing.

¤¤¤

November 1

I read that custom Halloween masks made of fiberglass are selling for up to $5,000. Wolverine faces, for instance, run from $699 for the cuddly type on up. In the local bank, taste runs more to cute little devils. Nobody says boo.

Trick or treatment.

The doctor is short, brisk, wears a bow tie. My CT-scan film is clipped to a light box on the wall. The examining room is a room without shadows. The doctor points with a thin finger. There's a large gray mass in my midsection. There's a blob pushing up against the abdomen wall—that's what I've been feeling. The blob surrounds the aorta. The blob looks immense.

"We can melt that away," he says crisply. I'm led to believe they do that all the time.

I feel a load lift off my mind and a breeze blow through.

¤ ¤ ¤

IT'S THE DAY before the election, and the *Times* reports that when asked that penetrating question, "How are you feeling?" Karl Rove said, "I'm feeling good. I'm feeling very good."

As good as Rove feels, I'm feeling bad, though Tylenol helps. When I lean forward, the cramp hurts more. When I lean back, I want only to shut down and sleep. My greatest pleasure—my only pleasure—comes as my consciousness spins down, the window of my awareness shrinks, like a lens closing down, iris-style. The smaller my world is, the more sublime. Narrowness is all—

Gingerly, I fondle the bulge in my abdomen. Then, even more gingerly, my testicles. I suddenly realize how tender they are. I'd lost interest in them, so it took me till now to catch on. I'm afraid to touch any other part of my body for fear of what I'll find there.

Lymphoma is like a rolling coup d'état. It's like the lower Manhattan skyline that stands there, an inflamed husk. Every time I'm anywhere in the vicinity, I can smell that hideous stench again, and taste the unending agony, and the horizon is full of the absence of the Twin Towers, and never mind how ugly the towers were, they were solid, they occupied space, I took them for granted, so did everyone else, they *existed*.

I'll be a hole in the air, a memory. I can be melted away.

It's not that I'm afraid to die. Nonexistence is nothing to fear. It's that I'll miss—something. I'll miss everything. I'll be among the missing. But of course that's a rotten way to put it. I'm morally damaged to think such a thought.

I can see how illness might lead some people to resentment and even vengefulness. Revenge, a motive for egomaniacs who set out to poison the future.

¤ ¤ ¤

PRO FORMA, I arrive at the inescapable dumb question: *Why me?*

And the inescapable answer is: Why *not* me? The follow-up question is: *Who else, then? My wife? My child? Somebody else's wife, husband, child?*

This way lies idiocy.

And what is so wonderfully sweet about the grapes I won't be plucking?

The banality of a reaction is a tribute to the fundamental nature of a fact.

This is happening.

I will be appreciated. I won't even have to finish my book.

No, I'm not afraid. But I *am* getting furious.

"It's infuriating, but all my reactions are boring," I say to Melanie.

There's still a chance that what I'm suffering from is an infection from India. Now for the biopsy.

¤ ¤ ¤

"WE CAN MELT that away," he said. You have to love a profession that practices optimism and has reasons for it.

¤ ¤ ¤

WHEN I COME back to myself, my belly is shaved, and my skin (except for two little bandages, one over my navel, the other northwest of it)—my skin is as smooth as a baby's bottom.

I'm regressing to infancy.

My body was once my plaything. It surprised and delighted me. Now it surprises and repels me. My midsection sags at the best of times. As I passed sixty, as if on cue, little cones of flesh began to appear around my vestigial nipples. I noticed it while playing ping-pong with my agile daughter, caught her eyeing my chest with the deniable pity of the young who have nothing to fear and all the time in the world that is the only world they know, which is their own. I don't share Nietzsche's zeal for mountain air. My feet prefer the ottoman. I'm imprisoned within this flabby carcass-in-waiting, and if that weren't bad enough, now it's gone out of control.

But self-pity is emotional flab.

⌑⌑⌑

I WAKE UP in the middle of the night, mind racing like a wheel in sand, spinning, stuck, going nowhere but deeper. And why, pray tell, is deeper supposed to be better? Nietzsche's Zarathustra: "The world is deep." But in *Beyond Good and Evil*: "Everything deep loves masks." And: "When you gaze for a long time into the abyss, the abyss gazes back into you."

⌑⌑⌑

THERE IS A new age cliché that goes: "Your body is talking to you." OK, I'm all ears. But I'm not getting the message. My cells have clammed up, or else I have gone stone deaf and am thrown back into a scatter of memories: snowy lawns and sleds, egg foo yung and stars, daydreams and occasional facts.

I'm skipping home from the Chinese restaurant with my little friend and neighbor Gail. It's night, and we skip down the sidewalk ahead of our parents. When we get to the entry of our building, she ties her invisible horse to the chain that keeps people off the lawn.

A big smile from the courtly waiter named Frank at Dominick's, an Italian restaurant in the Bronx, the place we go on special occasions. Huge hamburger steaks. Little tortoni in paper cups, vanilla ice cream topped with macaroon crumbs.

There's the vast, star-filled sky seen from the playground where I stop on the way home from Hebrew school.

There's the fantasy that I go downstairs to watch TV with Gail and when she opens the door she's wearing a sheer red negligee.

¤¤¤

MAYBE I WOULD hear my body speak to me more distinctly if I could silence the inner noise. The bodily pain is the least of this torment. It's the cacophony, the sum of all the shrieks, the frantic I, I, I, I that needs silencing.

At least it is tumultuous, it is acute and intense, it is *feeling*.

Nietzsche, right on the money again: "To talk about oneself a great deal can also be a means of concealing oneself." Could say the same about memory: a wild goose chase that starts out from an untenable present.

But why not conceal oneself? "Everything deep loves masks."

¤¤¤

THE WARP OF time. Time does not progress evenly, not at all. It shimmies, bends, accelerates, slows, stalls, doubles back on itself. Present time hooks up with earlier time and leaves interim times in the dark, sealed up, as if the intervening pages were glued together. Before time *t,* I was one person, and at time $t + 1$ I am—who? Not someone else, exactly, but someone on the wrong side of a precipice, looking back up at another self left behind irretrievably atop the opposite cliff.

Before I got sick, my night reading was Hardy's gorgeous, ungainly *The Mayor of Casterbridge.* Every night I looked forward to easing myself into that harsh cycle of grief, regret, attraction, repulsion, renewal, and loss. Just when the reader thinks the plot is heading along in a straight line, a woman walks in and gives the compass needle a flick. There was a practical motive for Hardy's plot lurches: to cook up suspense for the next magazine installment. But there was also an intrinsic plot pattern: Each time Michael Henchard thinks he's found an exit from the awful fate he fears, the exit twists. Each salvation mocks him. I followed Hardy's loving depiction of Henchard's gathering doom with joy and dumb hope.

Now *The Mayor of Casterbridge* gathers dust on the bed table, and I'll leave it there. Against all the mortality weighing me down, fictional lives seem lightweight, concocted, remote. In fact, even when I was well, or passed for well, I was already impatient with the fluff of much of what passes for fiction. Too often, just as I am supposed to be reading along seamlessly, I observe the sweat breaking out on the novelist's brow as he, as she, strains to become invisible, to adhere to the impersonal rules of character, plot, pace, etc. etc. When it comes to stories, I demand weight, heat, intensity—the full texture that yanks experience up by the roots, lifts it up, and demands, *Take a good look, feel it, chomp on it, you've never been here before.* Whether the book has fat characters, thin characters, round characters, flat characters—none of that matters. Those are the conventions of a thin two or three hundred years of human history—a flyspeck of time. Whatever the reviewers say, whatever your book group says, there are no rules—*none*—to mark out what is to qualify as a "novel."

Whether the plot is "plausible," whether the characters "develop," whether the conflicts are evident—all that fictional artifice matters less, or not at all. If, contrary to fact, I were well—the sound of those words is velvet and pain: *If I were well*—if I were well, I believe I would *still* long to read a book that doesn't resemble any other book, a book that takes chances, a book that makes up its genre as it goes along. I would not demand that the characters be "people I like" or even "people I can relate to." It would be a novel not because it matches the herd's formula for a novel, but because I judge it *novel*—a bringing of news, a gift of something I didn't think or feel or judge before.

Be that as it may. Right now, my own story is all the story I need, or want, or have room and stamina for. If I have room and stamina for it at all. My breathing is shallow; my feelings are mud in my lungs. I think what I feel is mainly grief and anger—make that rage. But I'm not exactly sure, and this is a disturbing truth about myself. It's embarrassing to be an emotional illiterate. That's what I've been most of my life. But am I also a trifle *relieved* by this torment, since ordinary living is *so fucking hard for me*? My feelings are blurred, melted together. I'm dumb with confusion.

¤ ¤ ¤

Election night, November 2

I turn off the election returns at a point when Ohio is still in the balance. The thing inside is pressing at my swollen belly and there's no one inside begging to be born.

¤ ¤ ¤

November 3

Strangely, I awake cleansed, my mind sharp, my skin alive, as if I've just stepped out of a warm shower. The air is my custom-made garment.

But not so fast—I have not reached the end of time, and there is a sequel. After a moment of virtual bliss I remember everything, *everything*. Everything that has happened, has *happened to me*, is going to keep on happening *to me*. The whole dead loss.

¤ ¤ ¤

BUSH WON THE popular vote by three million. Insert rant here.

⌑⌑⌑

WHAT HAS HAPPENED to me? What happens to me? The *what* that happens to me, the entropy, the deforming—

Now all breaks down. All. Breaks.

I know only panic. Panic knows nothing. Panic opens into a prospect of absolute damage, damage without measure, insults without measure—all-corroding, shape-shifting damage—this swollen, space-filling, bulging mass under my skin assaults all the gods, not only Apollo's reason but Dionysus's pleasure—hacks away at pleasure, snaps reason—breaks down everything orderly and compact, *everything*, dams the flow of the life force, swarms wherever it will, invades whatever it was that I was pleased (not so long ago) to consider myself—sprawls, crawls, decomposes—I disband—I'm a blizzard of out-of-controlness, explosions igniting explosions, unbridled fission—a crazy freedom to resist all the ordering hope I can throw at it—In me, in here, the parasitical growth, the cancer that is not me but depends on me, unbounded and formless, a haywire ooze, a molten haze, a mob of cells without character, without boundary, without stop—devouring chaos that spills out over the frame, raging, consuming—like these sentences that hardly begin and refuse to end, maelstroms of lava, labyrinths that are all boundary and cross-purpose—The future is all rough edges—

Not death but *my death*.

But first, the erosion, the decomposition, the seepage.

¤¤¤

BECAUSE DEATH IS inscrutable, we substitute stories.

The blob in my gut . . . M y G o d ! . . . It's a l i v e. . . .

What is it, professor?

I d o n ' t k n o w. I t ' s v e r y s t r a n g e. W e ' v e n e v e r s e e n a n y t h i n g l i k e t h i s b e f o r e. . . .

My life as a sci-fi horror flick.

¤¤¤

I AM PERFECTLY well aware that to take the election personally is a narcissistic maneuver, and a vulgar and pathetic one at that. And yet, I want to *put it all together*. What's inside me is outside, what's outside is inside, and I'm skating along the edge of a Möbius strip, trying to *hold it all together*.

Meaning, I'm trying to inject grandeur into my self-pity, the least impressive trait in the world.

Grandeur! It's a bluff. Cancer is calling me on it.

¤¤¤

I AM NOT purged.

From *Beyond Good and Evil*: "Whoever fights monsters should see to it that in the process he does not become a monster."

Here comes the hot, smelly breath of shame.

⌑⌑⌑

AND THEN THE fluorescent hum of a doctor's examining room. Sequestered from the world. As if I've been kidnapped.

Biopsy report: Lymphoma. Definitely.

The enemy has a name. This is satisfying.

⌑⌑⌑

NIETZSCHE, *GENEALOGY OF MORALS*: ". . . sickness is instructive, we have no doubt of that, even more instructive than health."

Instructive? I cringe and invite my soul.

⌑⌑⌑

November 4

I start calling and e-mailing my friends.

"It's OK," I tell Julia. "I'm not afraid. I've had a good life."

We were graduate students together. Lithe Julia who in the end preferred dance to philosophy, and ended up running an aerobics studio. She and I were lovers, later, for a while. I was melancholic and she was generous—there was, for example, a burst of ecstasy as we leaned against a tree near the Palace of the Legion of Honor. But we were better as friends. Beneath her California benevolence is the canny tough-mindedness that comes of having parents who were exiles. Her father, an Austrian Jew from a town called Judenberg, an anarchist who fought in Spain and did underground work against the Nazis, got out while the getting was good and made his way to China, did war relief, there fell in love with a woman from a village way out west. They ended up in Chicago, where Julia grew up, and eventually moved way out west again, bought some land, opened a hotel in Lake Tahoe, and Julia's mother learned to beat the pants off the locals at poker.

Julia urges me to visualize the tumors melting away. Well, why let the silliness of this idea stop me? If there is a will to power, why not a will to health? Here goes Pascal's wager again, dressed up for the twenty-first century. What have I got to lose? I color my tumors rosy, cut them into doilies, and imagine a colorful meltdown. I keep up this scenario for a few days. It feels more and more forced. So I let it go, though with a twinge of fear that haughtiness might be depriving me of a cure.

VISUALIZE WHIRLED PEAS, said a Bay Area bumper sticker. Moral: Don't lose your sense of the ridiculous.

¤¤¤

JANE, WHOM I used to live with, and whom I saw through her own cancer, tells me about people she knows who've weathered lymphoma, with or without recurrences, for fifteen or twenty years.

We think with odds and feel as singletons.

¤¤¤

SOME IDEAS OF what to do with a truncated life:

- Have an affair.
- Find somebody who's gotten away with murder and murder him.
- Feed the poor, tend to refugees, or otherwise do good.

In each case, there's the problem of the morning after, for which there's no pill.

I'm not a Christian. Why should I care about redemption at all?

¤¤¤

THE LAST TIME I met somebody at a dinner party and told her I was a philosopher, she smiled a little cat-smile—the little lines around her mouth switching like whiskers—and said, "But you're too tall."

That's what we get for being invisible—philosophers, a clandestine army of dwarves.

I thought this might be an innocent flirtation, or not so innocent, maybe, but it turned out that my height was all that interested her.

¤¤¤

"WHAT'S A PHILOSOPHER?" Natasha once asked. She must have been in middle school. She collected vocabulary the way other girls collected dolls.

"Why do you ask?"

She blushed.

I asked her about that, too.

"One of my friends said it's a guy who has lots of girlfriends."

"That's a philanderer, silly," Melanie said. "You're funny."

¤¤¤

WHEN I WAS a kid, one of my mother's friends said to me one day:

"How come your head is so small?"

"It is?" I replied, suddenly worried.

"It certainly is, considering how much you've got crammed inside it."

These so-called adults were always teasing me because of how much I knew, or how much they thought I knew, which was possibly because of how little they knew. Grown-ups getting their kicks by disparaging kids or turning them into freaks—some spectacle.

¤¤¤

I HAVE THE sensation that my head has swollen; it's heavy with years. It feels like a wrecking ball. My legs are dead weights. My balls are huge—the indignity!

My body is stone-heavy but also feather-light. My life is provisional. It always was, of course. Lucky me, I've struck pay dirt—the truth of things. It's all I can do to get my fill of that truth—to pack my time tightly, like damp sand—to inhabit my world—breathe my breaths. I'm crazy for all the air I can cram into my lungs.

Peculiar to say so, but I'm a happy man.

⌑ ⌑ ⌑

November 11

When I call Julia back, she says that after our first conversation she cried for two days, because I sounded as though I was getting ready to die.

⌑ ⌑ ⌑

November 17

I get a different scan, called PET, which produces a three-dimensional picture of cellular activity. I get jabbed with a radioactive isotope. Then, after an hour, I'm slid into a machine, inside which I generate a map of my tumor at work. PET, CAT—it's all so cozy.

Finally I will get to meet the doctor who will treat me.

My appointment's at four, at Memorial Sloan-Kettering, a tasteful fortress of treatment, salvation, and dying on the East Side.

We wait.

We are moved, Melanie and I, to an examining room.

A doctor, a "fellow" who trains, apparently, by doing the secondary work, comes in to poke me. He's impassive, but I'm comforted from the laying on of hands. It takes so little to convey care, and matters absurdly much.

At six-thirty, I'm still waiting for Dr. Berg. Melanie sits nearby, reading *Tess of the d'Urbervilles.* But no harm done. My consciousness has the consistency of sludge. Time stalls.

Finally there is the click-clacking of high heels outside the door. It turns out she's been waiting for the PET scan report, which has finally arrived.

"Diffuse large B-cell lymphoma," she says, not exactly cheerful, not downcast either. I ask her to repeat. She repeats. She feels for swollen glands under my arms. Nothing there. Now for some good news: The disease probably hasn't crossed my diaphragm. Now for the magic words:

"It's treatable and curable."

"My balls are swollen," I say.

She feels inside my pants. "And we haven't even been properly introduced."

I like this woman. I will trust her. She wears high-narrow heels and is improbably youthful and pretty, with a dark

Jewish perm—it comes as a surprise that she has three children. On her web site, she looks about sixteen.

She majored in mathematics at Princeton. You want your doctor to be precise. You want her to make a crack at Bush's expense, which she does. I don't want a monopoly on the sarcasm in my life.

I get dressed. We move into her office. She explains that I have three choices. Plan A, the "gold standard" for this type of lymphoma, consists of six rounds of a chemotherapy cocktail called R–CHOP, administered every three weeks. Plan B is a demanding chemo routine that requires long hospital stays out of town—not an attractive proposition. The results there are said to be stupendous—actually too good to believe, since the population getting the treatment includes HIV-positive and AIDS sufferers. She suspects this population is being cherry-picked to jack up the numbers.

In Plan C, I enroll in a "protocol"—not the one said to have been issued by the elders of Zion, but the technical term for a study under way at Sloan-Kettering. I get four outpatient treatments of R–CHOP, but at intervals of two weeks—they pack it in. Then there's a pause for CT and PET scans. If those are negative, fine, we know the R–CHOP has accomplished its mission and proceed to phase two: three treatments of a different chemo cocktail, called ICE, also at two-week intervals. These require long drips and thus, each time, two-night stays in the hospital. Various awful side effects are possible.

Logically, the protocol should produce better results than R–CHOP alone, since ICE operates on a different principle. So I'd be getting two different treatments, in sequence, and they overlap in their effects. If R–CHOP has accomplished its mission of wiping out detectable cancer cells by January (the PET scan will tell us), then we proceed to shoot up with ICE to prevent any future cancers from adhering to the cells. . . . Or something like that. The explanation sounds pleasingly logical, but I'm not sure I take it in. My head is not exactly there in the room with Dr. Berg, though it's not exactly anywhere else, either.

What are my chances? Do I want numbers? Will numbers make me feel better? Worse? Wiser? She's got numbers galore in her databases. I wouldn't have asked for numbers, but I'm not going to flinch at them, so a little reluctantly I say, "OK, show me some numbers, please." She pokes around on her keyboard. I belong to the category "high-intermediate risk" because I have four negative factors: The disease impairs me, I'm sixty-one, I've got an elevated LDH enzyme, and I'm at Stage 3, meaning that the disease is in two sites: There's some spread through the lymphatic system. But things could be worse: The marauding cells could be T-cells instead of B-cells, for example. CHOP by itself cures something like 55 percent (cure being defined as freedom from cancer after five years). R–CHOP by itself takes you up to something like 60 or 65 percent. With the extra ICE, the study's only been going for a year or so, but the numbers are excellent as far as they go—almost everyone's in remission, disease-free.

A year is only a year. But a year *is* a year.

If all goes well, I'll be done with chemo by the end of February. If not, there are forking paths—another biopsy, followed by two rounds of ICE, followed by one round of RICE (souped-up ICE), and a transplant of my own stem cells, etc.—arduous, risky. She hands me a flowchart.

I wish I hadn't heard the numbers. For a moment I feel as if I'm suffocating. But the phrase "good results" lifts my heart a notch.

"By the way, my mother had non-Hodgkin's lymphoma, too, three years ago," I say.

"It's not genetic," says Dr. Berg.

"She's fine now," I say, irrelevantly or not.

"Good."

Under Plan C, chemo starts in a week, phasing in gradually with half the first R–CHOP treatment the day before Thanksgiving, the second half the day after.

After a month in rousing pain and deadening anguish, I'm stagnating no longer. Medicine is more than science; it's action. Precarious joy is joy. I'm under way.

⌑ ⌑ ⌑

THERE'S NO ONE else in the elevator with Melanie and me and it's dark outside; traffic is streaming homeward, or toward duty, or entertainment, or food, or drink, or assignation, or joy, or fatigue—the destinations of my fellow New Yorkers, with whom I will get to spend a while longer, whether they care or not. We will go our ways on the same island, seek our separate intensities while breathing the same air, feverishly share the same . . . indifference. Yes, this is the essence of Manhattan: shared, sublime indifference in a minor key. I'm entitled to this conceit. It's authentic. Never mind that when other people unknown to me were the ones who had just been notified of their own reprieves, I was blasé. New York is all fitful energy and diffuse consideration but not much for ceremony. It has not been my mission in life to be more compassionate than everyone else.

It's past eight-thirty. The hospital is far advanced toward general slumber. We find three or four ground-floor exits locked, dart around like obstructed rats, and finally make our way to a lobby and exit the hospital onto the sidewalk on the York Avenue side. All the cabs streaming by on the near side of the street are occupied. Finally a cab sporting a dome light approaches heading uptown, on the far side of the street, so without hesitation I head into the street to flag it down.

A car honks and sweeps past me as if I am the toreador and it is the bull. I suddenly understand that I'm crossing against the light. I've walked into a stream of moving traffic.

But I'm reprieved! I can cross against traffic! I can walk on water! The world has lost its solidity, or I have. I'm ectoplasm. I'm pure will. I rise above impediments. I walk through steel. By definition, I have the right-of-way. I'll go my way and I'll get my way—right.

I'm reprieved and stunned, having taken leave of my senses, in other words. Bewildered, I lurch back to the curb. Melanie scolds me: "What do you think you're doing? Are you out of your mind? You just walked into traffic! Jesus!" She is merciless.

I abase myself suitably and try moving on with "How *are* you?"

"Don't you ever—" Her eyes light up with dark fire.

"I promise. How *are* you?"

She shudders. "I'm—OK. Do you think you're invulnerable? I can't believe—What's wrong with you?"

I hear an interior voice proclaim melodramatically: *I'll never be invulnerable again.* Then add: *I never was invulnerable in the first place.*

"Will you promise me not to scare me to death?"

Too quickly, I promise. The interior voice: *It's too late for that.*

We agree to leave it at that. Nietzsche: "A married philosopher belongs in *comedy.*"

We slide into the cab and sweep uptown, then left on a side street. I call my mother in Florida and give her my upbeat lymphoma report. She takes it in stride—she's an old hand at lymphoma. Then we jolt forward as the cabbie brakes too late and smacks into the car in front of us. The squealing of tires, the denting of bumpers, angry words on the street, and I don't care. I'm almost jubilant. I've got a diagnosis, a doctor, dates, plans. My life is whole. What else besides comedy does a man need?

We can melt that away.

¤ ¤ ¤

November 18

The haze of coming out of a dream—

I'm slogging uphill along a twisting road in bright sun high in the mountains above a town that registers on me as Berkeley, though it doesn't look like the actual Berkeley of tawny hills and cute cottages—I've got all the time in the world and no exact destination—There's a mild scent of sage, a feeling of remoteness and altitude, a puff of cumulus cloud hanging just off the sidewalk—On the opposite side of the street, immense ramshackle houses with Victorian facades pushing up against one another—Through a garden of ice plant and down a few stone steps I enter a big house, pass through a narrow corridor—The floor creaks—There's a fine stone Buddha and ethereal lace curtains in pale light—And then somehow, without having stepped back out onto the street, I'm out on a small patio where I make a right-angle turn and step into a different house, this one with narrow corridors and high ceilings, rooms festooned with plastic flowers—then into an open, dusty space in which stands a piano with only white keys, framed photos of graduates wearing mortarboards on top—

All the colors are muted now—I make my way out of one house and into another, through one corridor after another, all interconnected, into narrow, musty rooms that are not exactly inhabited, they're like museum reconstructions—I'm puzzled to find myself in this world of passages, houses upon houses, but I'm neither troubled nor frightened. Most of all, I'm curious—Where exactly am I, and where am I headed, if anywhere? I make my way through this warren, hoping to avoid any inhabitants, and indeed, I succeed in never meeting another soul, until I emerge into a big open area that resembles a campus—not exactly the University of California, but similar, with the buildings more widely spaced, as in a child's vision—

This can't be a memory, because I've never seen anyplace like this. So it's a dream, or began, at least, as a dream. Now I can summon it up at will. It has a hold on me. I'm wandering in new territory.

⌑ ⌑ ⌑

I CALL BARRY, who confirms that Plan C is the right call.

⌑ ⌑ ⌑

November 20

A letter from my Israeli friend Danny:

Alan my dear,

my first feeling was a shock. yesterday night was worse than a sleepless night. it was full of dreams, i woke up and fell into another dream—my kids appeared in the dreams, my parents, doctors, medical treatments.

my second feeling—this morning—is: it is a fight. you should win it. it is no time for sentimentality, not even for many sentiments. in any case the sentiments are too hard to be grasped at the moment. it is not very different from a state of war. i remember that in the one war that i participated in—the six day war—and in those that i remember as a civilian—feelings are of second importance once the real fighting begins. a kind of mobilization of all energy comes to the actual fighting. all the rest—including emotional balance—is delayed. it is a battle. and you have been in battles, hard ones. and the most important element of the battle is the professional knowledge: "treatable and curable." that should be your motto, and my motto, for the coming days and nights, and for the difficult hours that for sure will come: "treatable and curable." you will need all your energies. not one milligram of energy should be wasted now on any other direction but the direction of the investment in the process of curing, via the chemotherapy, and in the strong knowledge that the treatment will lead to full cure. there we are, and at no other emotional place: at the fight, and at the well-founded hope.

¤¤¤

"HOW *ARE* YOU?" I ask Melanie.

"I'm—OK. Intense. Time opens up. We have a plan. I'm alive. I feel alive. Like you. It doesn't get much realer than this."

¤¤¤

YOU CANNOT DESPISE your illness. It doesn't despise you: It takes you as a worthy antagonist. Respect your enemy.

¤¤¤

MELANIE HAS BORROWED a lightweight DVD player for diversionary purposes during my "infusion." I rummage among our household possessions, trying to figure out which movie to take to the hospital. Kieslowski's *Red*? Too sober, albeit inspiring. Herzog's *Stroszek*? Not too sober but not inspiring either. I'll have to order a copy of *Duck Soup*. For now, I'll go with *Casablanca*—once more, the heart-filling, eye-filling diversion for any occasion.

She goes online and there is an e-mail from prodigal Natasha, last heard from somewhere in Southern California, with subject line "I once was lost":

from the land of swine I greet u
appreciate your invite to land of fatted turkey
seriously has been 2 long & I miss u guys & agree
its time for a rendezvous so I can see your smiling faces :):)

My daughter is an original. I don't mean strictly her irascibility—I see too much of myself there. It's not her arch expression, which is altogether characteristic of her generation, perhaps also in expressing solidarity with her father, who appreciates this sort of mannered playfulness. There are a lot of kids nowadays who think they get to be original by having themselves tattooed or taking up an esoteric hobby like collecting albino dolls or adopting children from some Third World country. In Natasha's case, it's—what? Something I can't put my finger on.

Melanie charges into the bedroom in uncustomary tears and says, "She's coming!"

"For Thanksgiving," and my own tears outrun my anxiety. "Did you tell her—"

"Not exactly. I told her it would be an especially good time to visit because there are . . . developments."

"Funny, darling. Maybe she thinks there's a new building going up across the street."

"Whatever it takes," she laughs, brushing her tears away with the tips of her fingers.

¤ ¤ ¤

Wednesday, November 24

The chemo waiting room looks like the anteroom to a shrine, or an ashram, or a turban emporium. Everyone speaks in hushed tones. As in every shrine and casino, they're angling on hope. Things dance a little under the grim fluorescence, or my eyes are worsening, which can't be blamed on cancer—the ophthalmologist warned me about the next joy of aging, coming soon. In perpetual downtime, most of the faces are pinched and diminished. Some are blasé. So are the faces of the husbands, wives, daughters, sons, and friends who wait alongside them. I am a novice, wondering what I'm doing here, but others have the practiced, resigned look of knowing what to expect. Not long ago, they too were amazed to have been hijacked from what they thought were their lives—they were just walking along minding their own business—but they've evidently gotten used to the strangeness. The room is full of sagging and the averting of eyes. We've all stumbled into the same town of affliction, where everyone is a stranger, embarrassed to be here, awaiting a revelation that is taking its own time arriving. If this is war, I've flopped into the trenches at a time of general somnolence. It's a fight, but the enemy is within. You need weaponry, yes, strategy, logistics, all that, but you also need the intangible, invisible, possibly unconscious will to live. Most of the faces are wrinkled, but there is one thin woman, not much more than half my age, whose head is pale, gleaming, and bald.

I register at the far end of the waiting room. The young woman who takes my name and birth date—always the birth date; redundancy stops mistakes—wears silver hoop earrings and speaks in a comforting, slightly Spanish-accented voice, and measures out a disciplined smile, as if to say, we're all adults here, on the same plane, you don't deserve any particular pity, even "compassion." She refers to the chemo as an "infusion," as if it were something herbal.

Time is gelatinous. An attendant wheels a cart of sandwiches by. Peanut butter and jelly, tuna salad, cookies—comfort food, to go with the comfort paintings on the wall, the pastel landscapes. By the time she gets to me, she's almost out of peanut butter and jelly.

Eventually I'm ushered into a corner of the infusion room, where I stretch out on a long chaise, as if on shipboard to take the sun, but with a needle inserted into the skin on the back of my hand and a clear liquid dripping into my vein. The bony back of the hand is not where I expected a needle, but there is no doubt a reason.

For a good long while the infusion doesn't feel like much of anything. Melanie gets hungry and heads for the cafeteria. I close my eyes, impatient to sleep. Suddenly a chill comes up from the core of my body, and I'm freezing. I shake, out of control. I felt convulsions this intense only once before in my life, some thirty years ago, when I almost drowned under an overturned canoe during a river trip.

It was late fall, the wrong season, and no one else was on that stretch of the Russian River, maybe because the wind was gusting and it was blatantly a bad day to canoe. Outdoorsy Chris would not be deterred. I didn't much feel like making the day trip in the first place, but played along. The river, unusually high and swift at the launch point, got higher, swifter, and wilder. We careened into a fallen tree near the bank, and tipped, and capsized, and when I struggled back to the surface and found myself thrashing around in the air bubble under the canoe I realized that Chris's life vest had torn off. But I had enough crazy strength left in my free arm to grab her, hold her, pull her to shore. On the riverbank, in the direct sun, we lay on our backs shivering, gasping like fish breathing our last, or next to last.

I call the nurse, who says not to worry, that the cold spell and the shivering are signs that the infusion has started to work. The R–CHOP is smashing into the tumor cells. Trumpets! Alarums! All the silly prewar throat-clearing is over, the feints, the bluster, *la drôle de guerre*. The shooting war is on.

When Melanie comes back with her sandwich, I'm still shaking. The nurse takes her aside and tells her it's better that she wasn't here when I started to shake. Relatives often freak out at the sight.

I should be composing a dithyramb celebrating the jerky jazz-dance of Dionysian hand-to-hand combat that turns into revelry as the bodies twitch and shiver and overcome their death lust, which is their senselessness—in other words, their disease.

But I'm not Nietzsche, nor do I feel like carelessly dancing. Any Dionysian initiatives I attempt will have to do without benefit of the fermented grape or any other alcoholic support, all forbidden me for the duration of my treatment. I am going to have to face these months with lucidity—not my idea of a good time.

In the course of recent months or years, without ever noticing that I have passed any particular turning point, I have come to appreciate the power of the restorative twilight martini; or, during summers, the open-air gin-and-tonic; or, out at restaurants, the margarita or one of the hipper, sweeter, more exotic (if clichéd) martinis softened by apple, melon, or pear. In my old age, as I like to say, I have come to appreciate the incremental state of suspension or smooth evasion that arrives so readily and reliably as to expunge any guilty hint that intoxication must be earned by self-sacrifice. Drink has become my mistress—

I doze. That's my way. It's supposed to be hard to sleep while your body is in an uproar. For me, it's easy. I have no need of *Casablanca*.

¤¤¤

Thanksgiving, November 25

I sleep most of the day.

The doorbell rings in the early afternoon, startling me out of a sound sleep, and Natasha, my flesh and blood, strolls in and bursts into tears.

One thing that hasn't changed: She has the look of restraining herself, teetering at the threshold of a room she cannot bring herself to enter, as if she inherited her parents' respective airs of standing at odd angles to the world, but in a physical way. She's taller than I remember her, and paler, and more slender, and stands almost as erect as when she was a ballerina-in-training. Her lush black hair, as dark as her mother's, falls over her shoulders. Her eyes are the eyes of my own eager, wounded, inexperienced self. My older, yellower eyes tear up.

"Hey, you look good, Pop," she says half-convincingly, in a close approximation to her mother's clarinet voice, but speaking faster, in bursts, and using the same clarion tone that for years has seemed too big for her body. Why so loud? Is she telling her parents that we never listened to her? "You look good." Bless her and give her points for trying. She knows what part she's supposed to play—prodigal daughter delivering uplift. Her attempt is so earnest it touches me. At least she doesn't swallow her words, or pepper her sentences with "like," as the rest of her generation does. They, like, mumble; their actors mumble; and their heroes, if they had heroes, would mumble.

Never mind. I'm probably mumbling too. Even through my chemical haze, I'm thrilled to see my girl, and alert enough to be pleased that at nineteen she is making progress in the art of dissembling. Practice makes perfect.

She hovers over me, and as I lift myself a few inches off the bed, she gropes behind my shoulders and we clutch at each other.

"You look better, Natasha."

When she laughs, I can see that the glint in her tongue is a silver stud.

For a few moments the room fills up with my daughter's effort at cheer—as if the bedroom were a stage set, perfect and deserted, awaiting the moment when she would make her luminous entry, spotlit, because she is, after all, an audience favorite. But then everything goes quiet and the glow around her fades to black. She stands around clumsily, having forgotten her lines.

⌑ ⌑ ⌑

WHEN MY FATHER needed a prostate operation—I was eighteen or nineteen—I was away at college. I stayed away. I was studying and saving the world. I may well have made up some excuse about exams, but the truth is, I simply didn't want to visit. During my next trip home, for Easter break, he allowed as how his experience had been harrowing—he mentioned a catheter. I was apologetic and he was forbearing. I cannot remember what story I told myself. I was not proud.

Why did I stay away? Resentment is not pretty: It is only resentment, and can always give reasons, like alms. He hadn't wanted me to attend Harvard in the first place. (City College had been good enough for him.) It was my mother, out of her own savings, who covered the bulk of the cost, everything my little scholarships didn't cover. I didn't want to sully myself with hospitals. I must have had some idea about the relation between the prostate gland and the penis.

Forgive me, Father, I barely knew what I didn't do. He's dead more than fifteen years now. A heart attack, sudden death. I've come to resemble him, which is a pity because my mother was much more attractive, by which I mean more than that she had hair.

⌑ ⌑ ⌑

THE TURKEY IS free-range, the cranberries organic, the bread seven-grain, the wine zinfandel, but I'm going to have to get through depletion, fatigue, hair loss, myriad drugs, and Natasha's return without the ministration of alcohol. The best I can do is eat a few forkfuls, watch, and look forward to crawling back into bed. I extend my hand toward Melanie's plate, and she places her hand on mine and squeezes. I kiss the back of her hand. When she lets go, I pick up her wineglass and inhale from it. She laughs. When I am done, she lifts her glass (Natasha, looking stricken in my behalf, follows suit while I make do with water) and says:

"A toast to you, General Sternwood. Enjoy your recovery, darling."

When the infinitely dignified old (but was he older than I am now?) General Sternwood gives Philip Marlowe permission to smoke in the opening scene of *The Big Sleep*, what he says ruefully is: "I can still enjoy the smell of it. Nice state of affairs when a man has to indulge his vices by proxy."

A fogbank of silence moves in. I want to speak to Natasha of the moral worth of forgiveness (not on Christian grounds!), of the inevitable failure of all parents and the virtue of shipping out from the dead continent of the past, but I can't find any convenient way to broach the subject, so instead I try a smidgen of levity by telling a Bush joke, but it doesn't work. The conversation sinks like a deadweight. Natasha doesn't follow the news, or force herself to laugh at her parents' gestures in the direction of jokes. Nor does she inquire about the lymphoma. Melanie must have briefed her while I was sleeping.

"Natasha," I say after a long pause that has failure written all over it, in an effort to rescue our modest homecoming, "I'm curious about something." She gapes at me. "I've been meaning to ask you. Who would you say is your hero?"

Melanie likes to say that I relate to people by interviewing them, even my flesh and blood.

The only sign that Natasha has heard me is that her jaw slows down as she works through a mouthful of sweet potato. Melanie is silently cheering her on. Delicate little furrows form across Natasha's forehead before she descends into full scowl.

"An actual person? Could it be a literary character?"

"No fair bringing Tolstoy into this," I say.

She comes right back: "Why? You guys did."

"OK, but let's limit it to living persons."

"You are," she says finally. "My hero." And sounds like she means it.

"No, seriously," I say. "I wasn't fishing for that."

"I am serious. I mean really, does that come as a big surprise?"

"Well, interesting. I have to tell you, I think it's bizarre, but typical. When you ask your generation who their heroes are, if they don't name a sports figure or a celebrity, musician, whatever, they name a parent." Melanie is glaring at me with her *Drop the lecture* look.

Now I'm in too far to turn back. "I mean, after all, a hero is a personification of public virtue. A leader. A moral figure. Not someone you know in a merely private capacity."

Melanie doesn't have to ask Natasha to clear the table. She is relieved to get away.

When the pumpkin pie arrives, I ask her where she's been keeping herself. "Hanging," she says. "You know. Just hanging."

More or less where I've been, too. By the neck.

"Don't worry," she says briskly, "I'm not going to enlist in the Marines. I'm not at risk from online predators. I think the Internet is a dumb-ass waste of time. And by the way, am I done with this test?"

¤ ¤ ¤

Friday, November 26

Back to Memorial Sloan-Kettering for the second part of the first R–CHOP "infusion."

Now that the monster has begun to melt away, presumably, we're spraying the premises to make sure it doesn't come back.

Compact DVD player on my lap, I watch the first few minutes of *Casablanca*—up to Major Strasser's arrival at the airport and the pathetic I'm-here-too maneuvers of the Italian sidekick—then put it aside. It would be wiser to get a head start on Hobbes's *Leviathan*, which I have to teach the week after next. Ordinarily I would coast on last year's notes and college memories, but I need the extra homework, expecting to be in a muddled state. Though I have never been much for English empiricism, I appreciate Hobbes's methodical way of building up an entire system about the nature of human beings—theory of cognition, theory of language, and so on—before he gets to the rough stuff, namely, his theory of why we need to surrender ourselves to the all-powerful sovereign. It's not that I agree with his premises; it's that I take pleasure from the tight chain of his reasoning—there's a sleeping mathematician coiled in my brain.

Mozart's Jupiter Symphony takes over my mind. Music for chemotherapy.

¤ ¤ ¤

THE HOSPITAL SENDS me home with a whole pharmacopoeia of my own—pain pills, pills to prevent nausea, pills to avoid infection, pills to avoid constipation from other pills, and so on. Some I'm to take once a day, some twice, some three times; some in the morning, some at night; some for three days, some for a week.

And the pièce de résistance: I am to give myself daily shots of a drug called Neupogen for five days after each round of R–CHOP, the idea being to boost my white cell count to the point where it's high enough to be smacked down by the next round of R–CHOP—Sisyphus builds his own mountain. Shots into the upper thighs, left and right alternately. Pick up a syringe, take off the cap, jab the needle into a vial, suck down the contents, sit down, swab the skin with alcohol, grab a significant pinch of flesh, press the plunger, and shoot. Stow the used syringe in an empty milk carton. Keep track of the shots, along with the pills, on a special calendar with my name and the days preprinted. Don't dump the milk carton down the garbage chute, somebody might get hurt; bring it back to the hospital when you're done—

I get good at this ritual, drawing no more than a drop of blood each time. Afterward, a weird sense of pride and

years, I have mastered Socrates's ploys: the authoritative tone, the leading question, the tickling at definitions, the knowing gesture, the buildup of the straw man—but also the relinquishing of the authoritative tone at the right moment, the confrontation of one's own painstakingly built-up position with a counterargument out of left field, the earnest suggestion of outré but logical possibilities.

I nudge the discussion out of a few ruts by lavishing praise on the eighth- through twelfth-century Spanish Christian-Muslim-Jewish so-called Convivencia wherein Ibn Rushd and Maimonides thrived. The students perk up—they can appreciate conviviality, vitality in cahoots with other vitalities. In my experience, college sophomores were not passionately concerned with religious coexistence until 2001, when, for obvious reasons, they found themselves touched by awe and nostalgia on brushing up against the great, long-lost Spanish moment that was erased by the Christian Reconquista and the Inquisition. I emphasize the happy period of coexistence but also take note of the unfortunate 1066 massacre of the Jews in Granada.

We rumble along. Ibn Rushd of Córdoba thought it was fine to learn from the ancients—Aristotle, in particular—who preceded the advent of Islam. There were things to learn from pagans, he wrote. It was not their fault, after all, that they were born too soon to receive the proper and subsequent revelations. Ibn Rushd also thought God resided in the soul of man. How is this like and unlike Augustine's bifurcation of the world between the City of God and the City of Man? Discuss . . . etc.

And then my mind drifts, like AM radio at night, and these words show up: *I have cancer.* Then back to Ibn Rushd of Córdoba, he of the exemplary rigor and crystaline clarity, even if he devoted himself to resurrecting Aristotle, whose methodical genius has always left me cold. Aquinas, no slouch at systematic knowledge, called Ibn Rushd "The Commentator," but nevertheless I am left untouched by his "On the Harmony of Religion and Philosophy," written circa AD 1190. In his latter years he got in trouble with the caliphate.

Cancer has nothing to do with his circular reasoning or his touching ambition to speak meaningfully about the whole of creation.

I've doubled myself. I am two souls, but not in a way that either Augustine or Ibn Rushd imagined, or Mary Shelley either. Neither the teacher nor the man afflicted with cancer is more or less real than the other. Each is myself; each is incomplete. I toggle between the two. Does anyone notice that I'm doubled over from the pain in my abdomen?

Melanie sits in the corner, taking notes. She's decided to sit in on my class. She's catching up on philosophy and political theory, she says. I think she's afraid I'm going to collapse in the street.

Not so long ago, we visited the cavernous arched spaces of the Córdoba mosque, where Ibn Rushd must have worshipped. A few years later, the Christian armies marched in and converted it to the cathedral that it remains today.

This is no metaphor. Neither is cancer.

⌑⌑⌑

We can melt that away.

⌑⌑⌑

December 2

All around New York are provisional beings, the living and the dying. The living are dying; the dying are living. Look out the window and see them all, the doomed and the oblivious, scurrying, planning, anticipating. It takes a certain courage to refuse to know. The courage and idiocy of everyday life.

⌑⌑⌑

The deeply concerned look of acquaintances as they ask, with hurt eyes and lowered voices: "How *are* you?" (I even get it from people I've never met.) That most innocuous and banal of questions is now in dead earnest, even affectionate. Gossip can be a form of care. But when people radiate solidarity and scour my face for signs of my dwindling, they are also searching for signs of their own evanescence. I have become the abyss that looks back at them. They mean well, the healthy. Without doubt they mean well. If they didn't ask how I am, I'd resent it. But sometimes they plunge me back into the realization that I'm ill, maybe mortally ill, just when, for a moment, I had the luxury of forgetting, or pretending to forget. Is this their unintended purpose, to remind themselves of their health? Oh lucky, feckless humanity!

⌑⌑⌑

NOT THAT I need any reminding that cancer has taken up residence in me. There are the twinges of pain that penetrate the haze of the pills I take. There are the bookmarks that show up on my browser: Memorial Sloan-Kettering, lymphoma.org, WebMD. There's Barry's fat lymphoma manual on the bed table. When I see how much the treatments have advanced in the five years since he published the book, I take heart. Medicine is not an accomplished fact but an extended learning process. I benefit by coming along late in the game.

Natasha reminds me, too, just by being around. She's taken up residence in the apartment, like a low-lying cloud. The first flush of her return to the nest dissipates. Her spunk recedes, too, though not all her sweetness. Melanie says that she saves all her complaints and bad temper for her mother, that she wants to remain my darling little girl. A filigree of fine lines forms in her forehead. She mopes. She reads Agatha Christie novels one after another, sometimes two in the same day, as I did during a maximum spell of depression once, and told her I'd done, but was not especially recommending. (Who said children don't learn from their father?) She lowers her voice to the point where I have to ask her to repeat herself. Which she does, only slightly less unintelligibly. I decide not to ask her to clarify once again, since I wouldn't understand her next effort either and we would both be even more embarrassed than we already are. She's a foreigner. I start to interpret her sullen presence as less a gift than a gift certificate: *You're sick, old man. Watch me rally around you.* The married philosopher with children belongs in a *sitcom.*

But this could well be unfair. Maybe she's speaking clearly but I'm not receiving. Melanie thinks I should get my hearing checked. (I tell her I don't have time or stamina or, to tell the truth, desire to address all the forms of decrepitude that are converging on me—not now.) Natasha may not mean anything like what I think she means. What do I want her to do, anyway? Am I setting her up in a double-bind? If she were away, I would blame her for staying away. She's here, so I blame her for how she speaks, or who she is (and isn't). This sort of mindfuck might be the—or anyway a—reason she stayed away in the first place.

Melanie makes me promise that I won't ask Natasha how long she's staying, or when she's planning to look for a job, or go back to school, or how she's been occupying herself in recent months, or even what she's doing for spending money. I suspect that Melanie is subsidizing this stay. I don't want to ask. It's a measure of the strength of my will that I don't ask.

My daughter, my companion in sickness. We communicate with grunts and moans. What we communicate is something else. What we communicate is that we're making the effort to communicate. Which is something. A married philosopher with children belongs in *drawing room comedy.*

And a child carries her parents around like heavy, clanking chains.

¤ ¤ ¤

WHEN I TRY to imagine what she must be thinking, this opaque stranger with the brisk voice and the joyless smile, I come up blank. For all I know, her father's mortality is not an especially compelling fact of life, it's just background noise. For all I know, she's pining away for a lost lover (of indeterminate sex). For all I know, she's decided to teach English in Thailand, or take up importing the Central American folk art she always adored, or go back to school, or she has designs on the LSAT, or has lined up a summer internship at an absurdly overworking and overpaying law firm. The mind of Natasha is one of the known unknowns.

Melanie says we have to give her time. In principle, I agree. In practice, we've been giving her time ever since she started complaining about the required composition course during her freshman year, complaining that she was required to read—and if that wasn't bad enough, write a paper about—some incomprehensible gibberish that her instructor called Theory. (*Theory of what?* I wanted to know, but never mind.) I was patient when she complained that the whole lousy course set her teeth on edge, patient when she dropped out before registering for her sophomore year, patient when she announced that she was heading for California to "chill" and "clear her head." But sure, let's give her time. I've got time, if not all the time in the world.

She slides from room to room, staying out of my way, and there is a smoothness and dispatch in her movement—a residue of her ballerina poise. I can't help but wonder what all this time free of parental badgering is supposed to accomplish now that it didn't accomplish for her during her missing months. Or perhaps flight from her parents is just the inspiration she needs. I was a refugee from my parental home. So was Melanie from hers. It didn't kill either of us. Perhaps the collapse of the sheltering family is the great stimulus to becoming who one is. Nietzsche's father died before the boy was five. Perhaps this immense loss (followed a few months later by the death of Fritz's little brother) was the shock that catapulted him into philosophy. (He would have denied any tight cause-and-effect links.) When I speak of this to Melanie, she lifts her head, looks taut, as though she's about to snap, and I swear to God sparks fly out of her Mediterranean eyes in full daylight. "That's not very funny," she chastises me. I say that whatever else is going on with Natasha, where she's been, what she's waiting for, whether she's waiting at all, these are unknown unknowns, the ones that we don't know that we don't know.

"You're turning our daughter's life into a parable," Melanie says. I reply that she's right, but a good parable is worth a fistful of melodramas.

There is nothing in Natasha's demeanor to suggest that she is *not* brokenhearted in an old-fashioned way. When we pass each other walking down corridors, we hug wordlessly. I catch her mopping up tears. But much of the time she plugs herself into her MP3 player, lies on the sofa in the living room, if we permit her, or otherwise in my study, which doubles as guest room, on the pull-out bed, and takes long naps there, or grazes through her Agatha Christies. Sometimes she also pulls volumes of Nietzsche off the shelves. I find them lying around the room. I don't know whether this is for show.

I don't ask. I've stopped asking where she goes when she does go out. I weary of hearing her generic answer, "Hanging." Some walls are meant to be respected.

⌑ ⌑ ⌑

My daughter is trapped in speechlessness. I am trapped in words.

⌑ ⌑ ⌑

While Natasha is out, I step into my study to reassure myself that it is still mine, that one day I will have the desire to read again, and I see that she has left a copy of *Beyond Good and Evil* on the sofa with a yellow Post-it marking a page. Curiously, it isn't the hardcover from my collected edition but a badly creased paperback, possibly left over from her college year, when, come to think of it, she announced one day that Nietzsche was "awesome." I open the book and come across this, marked with a double asterisk: "A soul which knows that it is loved, but does not itself love, betrays its sediment: its dregs come up."

She left this message for me to find! She is telling me that she sees through me, that she knows that I do not love, and says so in a language I cannot casually reject—Nietzsche's language, the language of a man who (whatever he says) is incapable of a lie.

It must be obvious that I cannot find my way to her and she cannot find her way to me, and we are staring at two sides of the same wall.

But wait a minute. Is she thinking about herself or about me? Is this her confession? Is the double asterisk a sign that we're both at risk?

⌑ ⌑ ⌑

December 3

The way to keep insight from curdling into self-pity is by applying the cold compress of stoical detachment.

As the pain in my gut shrinks to an occasional twinge surrounded by memory, it's time to return to my researches into Nietzsche, and to wonder what I should do about him.

He himself made no secret of his maladies or how much he owed to them. "I feel that my real, philosophical task, to which if need be I shall sacrifice any career, is suffering," he wrote while still in his twenties. It amused him. "My neuralgia gets down to business so thoroughly, so scientifically, that it actually conducts experiments to see how much pain I can stand," he wrote Wagner. Even more, he paid tribute to his suffering. He was aware that he drew discipline from it: "My illness has been my greatest boon; it unblocked me, it gave me the courage to be myself."

I see him curled in a fetal position, with the light screened out. He calls Spinoza a "sick recluse," declares that Christianity starts with a "sickly excess of feeling," blames it for "confirming the rights of all those who suffer from life as if it were a disease," and with a great flourish of trumpets and a rousing *ho yo to ho* conjures up what would have to be called a *healthy* way to suffer from life. "The human animal is more sick, uncertain, changeable, indeterminate than any other animal, there is no doubt of that—he is the sick animal."

This furtive man who is driven to hole up in rooms that face north to reduce his exposure to sunlight and whose idea of a good time is a solitary hike in the mountains, carrying a parasol or wearing an eyeshade to protect his oversensitive eyes, scoffs at the resentful ascetic type who "loves hiding places, secret paths and back doors." He is always expressing "nausea"—"sudden nausea," "after-dinner nausea." This misbegotten, diminutive, shriveled, ulcerated, "three-quarters blind" (at age forty-three), or seven-eighths by another account, mistakenly medicated (the nineteenth century being one of the wrong centuries in which to be sick), and probably syphilitic misfit writes splenetically of the "repellent sight of the ill-constituted, dwarfed, atrophied, and poisoned."

How could so penetrating a mind—no less than the originator of genealogy, the notion that theories originate in specific down-and-dirty experience, only to get prettied up into abstractions long afterward—possibly have overlooked how central his physical misery was to his thinking? Some details in his own words. At age eighteen: "Congestion in my head." At twenty-six, he vents: "Oh how I long for good health! . . . [S]ome of my lower internal organs seem to be ruined. Hence bad nerves, insomnia, hemorrhoids, coughing up blood, etc." Later: "Chronic headaches of the fiercest sort, which lasted for days. Vomiting on an empty stomach, for hours on end. . . . Great fatigue, difficulty getting about, hypersensitivity to light." Even for public consumption, when he comes to relate his own version of his life, he writes of his "most profound physiological weakness," his "excess of pain." He confides in his loyal reader that he came to his exuberant breakthrough after resigning his professorship at "the lowest point of my vitality," a time when his eyes were so weak he literally could not see more than three steps in front of himself, a time when, "equipped with the strongest eyeglasses, he sat with his face almost touching his notebook on the lectern"—this was the reminiscence of one of his students. It was only at the end of his teaching career, "in the midst of the torments brought on by an uninterrupted three-day headache accompanied by the laborious vomiting of phlegm," that he could finally think clearly. (Has any other philosopher ever been honest enough to speak of the role of phlegm in his life?) It was then that he could see through to an understanding "for which when I am in better health I am not enough of a climber, not refined, not cold enough." Not enough of a climber! He is capable of six- and eight-hour hikes in the mountains, though to little lasting effect.

If the great booster of health weren't chronically sick, why would he have complained over and over again in his letters to his nearest and dearest? For example: "For years now I've lived somewhat too close to death and, what's worse, to pain. I seem designed for lengthy torment and skewering over a slow flame, and don't even know enough to lose my mind in the process." And: "At bottom I'm sick in the head and half-insane, completely confused by long isolation. I've arrived at this reasonable (or so I believe) insight into how matters stand after having, in desperation, taken an enormous quantity of opium." Evidently that doesn't work so well. He doesn't mention the opium again.

But he does identify sickness with intellectual timidity. Consider this, from *Beyond Good and Evil*: "Skepticism is the most spiritual expression of a certain complex physiological condition called in ordinary language nervous debility and sickliness." This pallid skepticism he contrasts with both robust doubt and rollicking affirmation. But having acknowledged that his state of mind is the "expression" of his damaged body, he proceeds to pin the damage on . . . race- and class-mixing! The fashionable pseudo-science of his time tells him that "hybrids" suffer degeneracy of the will. So Nietzsche succumbs to idiot racism and joins one of those herds for which he reserves his most scathing contempt. . . .

Here is my own preliminary, if obvious, diagnosis. My good Prof. Dr. Nietzsche, you suffer from a case of severe overcompensation, with complications. Suffering from vertigo, you compel yourself to skip up to the edge of the precipice. I see poor, pale, blinking Fritz jumping up from his desk, rushing off to the chamber pot to vomit and, in the midst of pure misery and stench, salvaging a cure: scorn for pity. (How he hated being the object of his mother's irrepressible pity for her adorable weakling!) And so he staggers back to his sickbed and dreams up the Will to Power, the human dynamic that—for fifteen minutes here, an hour there—triumphs over the immutable all-too-human fact of Powerlessness.

⌑ ⌑ ⌑

MEANWHILE, NATASHA REMAINS out of reach, but I am getting used to her presence, am even bemused by some of her habits (the way she tosses her hair and stops for a long look when she passes a mirror, the stylized scrawls of her name that she leaves on notepads lying around the study) though definitely not by others (the way she slams her cell phone shut when I pass nearby). But day to day, even hour to hour, the simple pleasure I took in her return fades, first into a state of quiet relief, then into nothing at all. I have to remind myself of my gratitude and goodwill. I know my obligations. But gratitude that requires all this labor isn't genuine.

In any case, how grateful is a sick man required to be? This is a question to ask when and if I'm no longer sick.

I propagandize on behalf of vitality but like an old hack of a crooner recycling romantic oldies in a piano bar, I don't feel it. I'll settle for longevity, that pallid aim, though it has become the national pastime.

I used to know what I wanted. Once upon a time, I wanted protracted and carefree sex, talent, good dope, and the admiration of strangers. Then I wanted occasional but still astonishing sex, varied wines, dry sherry, a Cuban cigar every couple of months, frequent lamb chops and sea scallops, high-grade ice cream, and adventuresome graduate students. I wanted to write a splendid book. I wanted a happy wife, a happy daughter, and a reasonable number of grandchildren whether happy or not. Now my life is stripped down to primitive elements, or actually one only: *I want to exist.* Of course, I also want to see how certain elements of our collective fate turn out. I want to rack up birthdays. I want to see if America wises up. I want to see who follows George W. Bush and how many pieces he (she?) can pick up. *I want to see how it turns out.* I am a character in a '50s melodrama. In truth, just like the Susan Hayward character stripped bare of her composure, I want to live! That's all! That'll do! I wait. That's my activity: suspension. As on a rope bridge.

¤ ¤ ¤

I'M WASHING MY hair in the shower and suddenly see strands of hair all over my shoulders. I let out a whoop.

"What did you say?" Melanie shouts.

"My hair's falling out! It's working!" I run down the hall, shouting: "It's working!" My Eureka moment. I'd been prepared for it, but there's still nothing like the evidence of the senses. The idea is that the chemo cocktail blasts the faster-growing cells—all of them. What's sauce for the tumor is sauce for the follicles.

Women say that the worst thing about chemo is the vanishing hair, the womanhood draining away. My mother bought herself a wig, in advance of her treatment, though she was reluctant to wear it, being convinced it was a poor fit. Not being a woman, I exult.

"You rule!" Natasha cheers.

¤ ¤ ¤

THE JOY OF having good news to broadcast. I want to call my friends—*Guess what? My hair's falling out!*

And more thrilling news later the same day: the realization that the wrenching pain in my gut has vanished. *We can melt that away*. I'm on the edge of tears.

Clear feelings with sharp boundaries, for once.

¤¤¤

December 4

Here's another clear feeling: the joy of a day without pain. The presence of absence is presence. Relief is belief. Relief is enough.

I prolong the joy by lying down on the sofa. I close my eyes and listen to Maria Callas and Carlo Bergonzi sing *Tosca*, over and over, their chocolate tones and balls of lightning spilling all over the room. Tragedy wells up from deep in the chest, and so does relief. This is my discount ticket to the realm of the spirit, an absolute eternity where emotions do not require any occasion, any strength, any body at all but the ability to pluck vibrations from the air. Yes, timeless! Yes, absolute! Today I claim the right to the sublime! Fortunately I do not understand Italian, so the sublime comes to me undistracted. The *utter* is freed of the *utterance*. The music is freed of meaning, as life should be. The way my existence is spared from meaning now that it is (perhaps) spared.

I forget myself. My exhaustion is earned.

Again, as when I was a child, sleep is a reward.

¤ ¤ ¤

MELANIE HAS JOINED the Museum of Modern Art and aims to visit there once a week. She's also subscribed to a jazz series in the Allen Room in the Time Warner building, from which she says there's a gorgeous view of Central Park. Keeping body and soul together. I will indulge my aesthetics by proxy.

¤ ¤ ¤

AT THE BEST of times, Melanie likes to say that I live in my head. "You don't know the half of it," I tell her. I keep rearranging the furniture.

But the time has come to goad myself into a walk around the block. It is my duty. Perhaps I will have a thought, or spot something interesting: a streak of light where winter sunlight strikes a water tower, or a sleeping baby being strolled around the neighborhood with the misleadingly self-sufficient look of the Buddha, or a spectacular sports car, or a button expressing deep and creative loathing for the commander-in-chief, or a reflection of myself looking stronger than I feel in a plate-glass window. Any visual epiphany will do. But I step with care, for I am prone to trip over the slightest unevenness of the sidewalk. The air is like cold glass pressing against me.

When I lumber back to the apartment building, Natasha is skulking in a doorway. She watches the addicts try to sell used books and comics from their card table, dragging smoke into her lungs as if she needed an excuse to breathe deeply, her skin wintry and sallow, looking for all the world like (as we used to say) a bum. She is altogether too fascinated by the men who live on the street.

"Hey," she says, avoiding my eyes, in what I have come to accept, even copy, as the approved form of greeting.

"Hey." As usual, I want to say something to her but I don't know what it should be. "See you upstairs."

I wonder if we can melt my daughter's lethargy away, or more to the point, whether she can. I head back to bed. A few minutes later, I hear her treading softly past the bedroom door (out of consideration? avoidance?) but I call her in.

She sits at the end of my bed, from which I appear less fearsome, I guess. She's in jeans, has one foot on the floor and the other crossed over her leg.

"So tell me," I finally say.

She will humor me. "Yes."

"I mean, tell me." It is unnatural that I should have the stammer and evasiveness of the child, not the confidence of the father. This mutual awkwardness frustrates us both, I because of what I don't say, she because of what she fears she will have to say.

Her eyes go all furtive and hunt around the room looking for a place to hide, or an exit, until she settles back on her elbows, gazes at the most remote corner where the ceiling meets the wall, and says with a little flicker of her lips: "OK, don't make me stand on a box wearing a hood, with my arms splayed out, anymore." She illustrates the pose. "I'll talk. What would you like me to tell you?"

There is a telltale pause as my daughter takes note, I hope, of how reluctant I am to push.

"What's going on with you?" I say finally.

"What do you mean, what's going on with me?"

"You know, your—plans."

"You know, visit my sick father."

"Well, yes, that's wonderful, but—"

We are like old chess players who have played the same opening so many times we can roll it out in our sleep—and we do.

She rolls her eyes. "Oh God, I hate this."

"Maybe if you talked to me, you wouldn't hate it so much."

The pleasure of condescending self-righteousness is matched by its impotence. But she pauses.

"You mean, it might be enough that I'm visiting my father who's got cancer?"

"Please, Natasha, you know how grateful I am. Sincerely."

"Uh-huh." When did we start to talk like characters in a B movie? How do we break out?

"If I haven't showed it, please forgive me."

"I forgive you."

"Thank you. But really, our obligations go both ways, and I've noticed that you don't seem to be in any hurry."

"That's because I can't think of anything to do that's more valuable than helping out around the house when my father needs all the help he can get."

"Thank you again, and do you mind if I ask what you're living on?"

"Would it matter if I minded? My savings. I have savings. I'm a good citizen. Want to see my bank statement?"

"Cut it out. I'm relieved that you have some savings."

We check each other out to see how far we can push this without detonation.

She breaks the silence. "I know the drill. Now you're going to ask how I happen to have earnings to save."

"The question did occur to me."

"I had a job." Then with a small smile: "It was nothing to write home about."

"Funny."

"And now you're wondering when I'm going to find another job. Or whatever."

"The question did cross my mind."

"You know, Daddy, I know this is all a monster for you, and I appreciate that you're restraining yourself."

"I don't think it's a picnic for any of us."

"No, not a picnic."

And I wait. I am not going to say anything about the stud in her tongue.

She bunches up her hair and tosses it to one side. She comes up with a rubber band and twists it around the ponytail, then twists it again. "You're always studying me," she says. "You could write a book about me."

She's right.

"Are you? Writing a book about me?"

"At the moment I don't have the energy to write any book at all."

"Well, there you are." She has probably noticed my non-denial denial. "Anyway, doesn't your hero Nietzsche think that work is degrading?" Her sardonic tone is about as easy to miss as a truck.

"Ha-ha. Not exactly. He worked like a maniac."

"He *was* a maniac."

Although my mind is limping and my tongue is thick, I have the impulse to tell Natasha what I really think: that she is in love with inertia, that she is a self-saboteur, that she wouldn't know a plan if it smacked her between the eyes, that she shares the drifty mood of her whole generation—excepting those who are planning to go to law school or medical school, in which case they suffer from a surplus of plans and a shortage of purposes. The thought crosses my mind that the reason she's staying with us is to flaunt her incapacity and so to punish her parents for daring to wish for more. Many erroneous, unfair, mean-spirited thoughts cross my mind.

I say only: "At the end, at the end. Before that, no. Or not exactly."

She weighs that. Should she take advantage of my weakness and try to get the better of me on my own subject? No, not that move, not now, not today. Instead, she reverses field:

"You used to say that if anything is worth doing, it's worth doing slowly."

That does sound like the sort of thing I used to say. More than once in my life I myself have fallen in love with inertia, that languid tease. During my protracted spell in graduate school, I spent many a wine-soaked evening filling the air with rationalizations and prating about the virtues of a life consecrated to contemplation. (Many too were the times I quoted Socrates to my bewildered parents, who were offended, reasonably enough, to be told that "the unexamined life is not worth living.") If I lectured my daughter to the effect that she should learn diligence before learning to subdue it, what would she say?

I bite my tongue. In truth, my thinking slogs along as if I'm fighting the gravitational pull of, say, the surface of Jupiter. I want to say, *It's lovely to have you home, Natasha*, but the words stick in my throat.

"Can I go now?" she asks. "Is the interrogation over?"

"For now. Sure."

¤ ¤ ¤

THIS EXCHANGE EXHAUSTS me. From such moments of venting comes no relief. Swallowing your hurt produces pomposity, and pomposity produces debilitation. No wonder the kings and queens were always seated on thrones. This must be why they were called blue bloods: They lacked enough red cells to jolt them off their bottoms.

Mysteries of Natasha: How can she be simultaneously wired and inert? How many hours a day does she sleep? Why doesn't she ever mention a boy? Is she a lesbian? Does she have tattoos in inaccessible places? What does she do with her mind?

Mysteries of Alan: Am I incapable of gratitude? Isn't it far, far better that she's here than if she were wandering the earth? How would I feel if she were a lesbian? Fine? Really?

Natasha, controlling herself, departs, and as I drift into sleep, I reflect that she is of course right about Nietzsche. From age forty-four on, he *was* a maniac—it is well to remember that the conventional wisdom is not always wrong. He was an unusually fluid, ingenious, and operatic maniac, but a maniac nonetheless who skidded out of control over the course of many years—the debate is about *how* many. Do I have the right to overlook the obvious? All his talk about self-overcoming is a disguise for his self-disgust, the self-disgust that takes the form of hideous migraines. Self-disgust is his will to power turned against himself. Natasha is guilty of a slacker form of self-blockage, but in truth, she learned to value weakness from me—even if I exalt it as "thinking against myself."

For all his ferocious energy before he collapsed, Nietzsche would surely have wearied of living if he had lived as many years as I. As he became more famous, he would also have become more misunderstood, and as his letters show, misunderstanding exasperated him. To go on suffering fools and rogues like his anti-Semitic sister would have worn him down. All frictions start out enlivening you and then wear you down. I would never want to argue that he deliberately went off his rocker, but it was mighty convenient that he did so before he had to face an actual life-threatening disease in the full light of sanity. I don't know how he could have kept up his morale if he had gone on living, especially as his line of thought gave every appearance of winding down. He needed to push his sanity to a conclusion, too. He certainly had moments when he could admit how desperate he was. "If I were not such a good example of a play-actor," he wrote to his sister, "I could not bear to live another hour."

He lived fast. He was a self-consuming storm that scattered ink as it ravaged the landscape—a landscape that was, in the end, also himself. I'm enthralled by Nietzsche—no, I *love* him—because I too want to be consumed, torn apart, swallowed up.

¤¤¤

I AWAKE FROM a long nap, refreshed, and head for the study to look up Nietzsche on the subject of work. Natasha was right. He's scathing. He deplores "modern, noisy, time-consuming, proud and stupidly proud industriousness." He laments the advent of "weak-willed and highly employable workers who need a master, a commander, as they need their daily bread." Work is for herds. What a writer does is something else—more like play.

¤¤¤

IT STRIKES ME that all three of my favorite archangels of nobility, fervor, irreducible freedom, and fierce will are essentially fatherless sons. Nietzsche was under five when his father died after a series of seizures that for almost a year had left him staring, mute, and immobile—the doctors called it "softening of the brain." Sartre was little more than a year old when *his* father died of a fever. Camus was an infant when his father was killed in the Battle of the Marne. Of the three, Nietzsche, who actually knew and remembered his father, was the harshest against authority, the stormiest, the most disturbed—he had at least a remembered father who took up residence in his mind. All sons must overthrow their fathers, but the fatherless sons find it easiest to feel the intoxication of freedom. They revolt against ghosts.

¤¤¤

NATASHA AT LEISURE. Natasha asleep. Natasha in flight. Natasha copping a smoke. I know I am an ingrate, but I still refuse to abandon my common sense and parental concern. As a failure, she is a success: She doesn't suffer from it, nor does she rejoice; she lies there, inert, a lump, not even resentful. Resentment would at least be an eruption of energy.

From *Ecce Homo*: "Sickness itself is a kind of ressentiment. Against it the invalid has only one great remedy—I call it Russian fatalism, that fatalism without revolt with which the Russian soldier, when a campaign becomes too strenuous, finally lies down in the snow. No longer to accept anything at all, to take anything, to take anything in—to cease reacting altogether." Of course you have to hand it to those Russian fatalists: They beat back Napoleon and Hitler.

Natasha loves her fate. One thing I'll say for—or against—myself: I don't love mine, unless we consider that chemo is my fate, in which case I embrace every last brutal molecule in a carload of R–CHOP.

⌑ ⌑ ⌑

ONCE IN A while, approaching behind the sofa where my daughter's body is sprawled, I feel the most abject love for this young woman. I reach out and squeeze her shoulder. Sometimes she stirs and places her hand on mine, sometimes not. I remember a little dark-haired girl in a snow suit. She looks out the window and spots "a lellow pluck." My father liked to talk about the day I looked out my own window, saw a truck, and called out, "Colonial Sand & Gravel," astonishing my parents, who didn't know I could read on my own. This marked the end of the time when they felt required to read to me. After years of therapy, which now that I think of it was little more than a series of follow-up exercises in ressentiment, I threw it up to my father that he had resented relinquishing his role as the man who read aloud to me, and made me feel guilty for depriving him of that role. He didn't exactly deny it. "Might be, might be," as he said about many things.

A wordless family might be the best kind.

¤ ¤ ¤

I SAY TO Melanie: "You know, I am very stupid about Natasha, but I really have no idea what she's doing here. Except, of course, that she loves me and she wants to show me that she loves me."

"Those are two reasons. That's a lot of reasons."

I stick my arm down into my sack of vocabulary and grope around, but cannot find an adequate name for my feelings.

"She's biding her time," Melanie says. "I think she wants to connect with us but she's afraid."

It's interesting how Melanie, whose strong suit is not patience, has nothing but patience for her inaccessible daughter.

¤ ¤ ¤

I TELL NATASHA that I was wrong about Nietzsche's attitude toward work. I hope this will spur conversation.

Behind her eyes I think I see a little flash of *Told you so*. But she shrugs, says "No biggie," and walks out of the room as if she has urgent business elsewhere.

¤ ¤ ¤

December 5

I grow stronger, fitfully less tired, as I grow steadily more bald. This is not a bad trade-off. It's curious how many types of exhaustion there are, once you start thinking about them. (You need to overcome the heaviest before undertaking the exercise.) There's black exhaustion, smoky gray exhaustion, and silver-streak exhaustion slicing through an otherwise black exhaustion. There's muddy exhaustion, watery exhaustion, Jupiter-gravity exhaustion. There's steady-state and stop-start exhaustion. I've come out of steady-state and moved into stop-start.

I start keeping lists of what to do if I survive:

1. Revisit India—caves, southern temples, and (briefly) an ashram. This time, pass up the chocolate mousse.

2. Be more helpful to my daughter. (How?)

3. Be kinder to my wife.

4. More sex and more loving sex.

5. Bewitch, dazzle, or otherwise coax students into surpassing themselves.

6. Make love on LSD.

7. Eat anything I want.

8. Drink anything I want.

9. Cultivate gratitude. I've had a good life.

10. Get down to the hypothetical book. Working title: *Nietzsche: The Health of a Sick Man.*

¤ ¤ ¤

TODAY, FOR THE first time since the diagnosis, I make it all the way to eleven-thirty in the morning before needing to climb back into bed or wincing from that percussive thought, *I have cancer.*

I want to get some air in my lungs, and drag my bones out onto the street, where I enjoy the sting of the light rain on my skin, and wander down Broadway beholding my fellow creatures in their daily state of grace, sullenness, pride, dismay, and perplexity. I don't need to crank up my will to exist. I exist—this is enough. This is not, perhaps, the most thrilling existence, but it is mine.

Even if I still look down every once in a while to see I'm at risk of stumbling over the rippling pavement at intersections—

rippling from too many repairs. At my age, watching my step is not such a bad idea, anyway.

When does a human being, too often repaired, start stumbling over himself?

¤ ¤ ¤

WITHOUT LOOKING AT the list above I write a new to-do list from scratch. Nine out of ten items overlap, though the order is different, and any or all of Vietnam, the Atlas Mountains of Morocco, and the Mayan pyramids of Guatemala substitute for India.

¤ ¤ ¤

MY AMBITIONS ARE feeble—beneath me. My ambition is now to imagine a greater ambition.

> *In vain have oceans been squandered on you, in vain*
> *the sun, wonderfully seen through Whitman's eyes.*
> *You have used up the years and they have used you*
> *up,*
> *and still, and still, you have not written the poem.*
>
> —JORGE LUIS BORGES, "MATTHEW 25:30"

¤ ¤ ¤

December 6

I looked into my heart and it said: Not yet.

¤¤¤

December 8

I dream that I'm walking across campus and suddenly realize that there's a second undergraduate course I'm supposed to be teaching this semester and I've completely forgotten about it. I left the students in the lurch. I'm flushed with embarrassment—and a twinge of fear: The powers that be will know that I'm delinquent.

The next thing I know, I'm giving a lecture in a dark hall with wooden paneling. Toward the end of the period, I dribble to a stop. I just fade. I simply don't know how to conclude. So I sit down onstage and start writing.

The students wait as I scribble away, but at some point they grow restless, standing up, one by one, and walking out of the hall. My heart sinks. I've lost them. I rationalize that I've taught them a Zen lesson about inconclusiveness.

Moral: I don't live in seclusion. Even when by myself, in the silence that is my favorite landscape, I'm in good company. Others are in the fight with me. My war is not private. I owe it to those who love me.

¤¤¤

Dear Danny,

Finally a little calm when school does not command my attention. . . . Your letter was very, very helpful. Yes, it is a fight. It is awfully important to me to feel that it is not mine alone. I really do have allies. I have not felt this so fully for years—if ever. Blessings come to me—everyday blessings. So my friendships are more vivid. Even my teaching is more vivid to me.

The physical effects from the first round of chemotherapy have not been so bad. My energy is pretty high. No bad side effects to speak of. The amazing thing is that the tumor has visibly shrunk—even within a few days of the first treatment. The worst of the fatigue is over (but that is pending the next treatment, which comes next Monday). I no longer feel simply hijacked, or kidnapped, by the disease. I now feel that the fight is on, a good fight, and it is not such a bad thing to live with, this fight.

¤¤¤

December 9

I dream I get a phone call from Marilyn Benjamin, who died of cancer a few years ago. I never knew what, if anything, to say to her. Now, for the life of me—for the life of me!—I can't remember what, if anything, she has to say to me. Communion without content.

⌑⌑⌑

MY WHITE COUNT must be rebounding. When I wake up from a nap, I don't long for another nap. It's almost time for me to report back to the hospital and get blasted again.

Natasha, chin high, strides into the study this afternoon and asks in a take-charge way if I've got a minute.

"I have nothing but minutes."

The second surprise: "I think I'll get Mom too." I traipse out of the study behind her. She heads for the kitchen, pours herself a full glass of white wine—in a water glass—stops at the bedroom, where Melanie has been catching up trying to salvage an overdue manuscript, and herds us into the living room. This is serious. Previous summit meetings were always called by Melanie or me, and sometimes we were doing the pouring, no doubt setting a bad example. Natasha is taking charge. She heads for a seat in the armchair that faces away from the window. She is letting it be known that she won't be distracted. The winter light behind her is threadbare, but there's enough backlighting to cloak her expression. Melanie and I sit on the couch directly across from her.

"OK, we're all sitting down," she says, scraping her chair back to retreat a few inches further away from us. "Suppose I were to tell you that last year at this time I was a drug courier for a gang of Jamaicans."

Melanie is dumbstruck. Natasha gulps wine. I want to know details. Natasha delivers details. On a temp job, Natasha says, she met a receptionist who never lacked for splendid clothes and drove a fabulous sports car, and let drop that she made $1,000 a month carrying marijuana. Natasha told herself she had nothing to fear because she hadn't crossed the legal threshold of eighteen. She met the boss, name of Elvin, at a mall, found him affable and businesslike, so signed up. She'd be delivering the goods to his brothers, sisters, and cousins, so there was no fear of betrayal. Once a month he would take her to a travel agent and pay cash for a ticket under the name she used on a fake ID. She would carry two small suitcases onto the plane. Each contained a brick of compressed weed wrapped in packing tape and trash bags, then in chemically aromatic sheets of Bounce, then in heavy wrapping paper. In a linen blazer and white linen shorts, wearing a headband, collegiate-looking, she was a shoo-in. Nobody gave her a second look.

When she went to the designated place in Detroit, Cleveland, Chicago, Boston, wherever, she exchanged the parcels for grocery shopping bags full of $20 bills, and two empty shoeboxes. She filled the shoeboxes, loaded them into the carry-on bags, took a taxi, stopped off at a drugstore, bought some hand creams and cosmetics, stuffed them into the suitcases along with the shoeboxes, bought a return ticket under her real name, flew back to LAX, and took a cab to Elvin's. He counted out $1,000 for her. They drank Moët champagne and toasted business prosperity.

That was the routine, once a week, for months. Elvin was unfailingly polite. He advised her to save money for college and to stay away from tattoos. He himself drove a plain-vanilla car, didn't wear jewelry, and sent money back to Jamaica. Professionalism, family values.

Natasha is calm, also professional. No downcast eyes, no staring off into space. She might as well be describing a summer vacation. Did she ever have a close call? Not really. Sometimes she would be told to open her suitcases and asked about the parcels. Sculptures, she'd say. Once, when a package was wrapped so tightly the X-ray couldn't penetrate it, the inspector told her she couldn't get on the plane unless she opened it. Natasha got huffy: "You can see it's not a gun!" "We're not just looking for guns," was the reply. Indignant, Natasha stalked away with her suitcases and rode off in a cab. Once she was free and clear, she started to shake.

And then there came a day when the superintendent at Elvin's building eyed her up and down in the elevator, looked at her suitcases, and guessed which apartment she wanted. That made her nervous. A few months later, the apartment was raided and one of Elvin's brothers fell from the window and smashed his skull. Bad karma was gathering. Then her friend the former receptionist got caught carrying money. That was enough. With no hard feelings, Natasha quit.

I'm still breathing. My feelings spin like numbers on a roulette wheel while I wait for the little ball to settle. I don't know whether I'm more aghast, relieved, or angry. Pirouettes of the unsaid, the better-not-say; whole ensemble productions of stalling. All our silences know each other's moves. To this point, I haven't taken Melanie's hand, because I don't want Natasha to think that we're in cahoots against her, but I take it now. My wife sits in anguish and judgment.

"So there it is," Natasha says. It is what it is, as everyone likes to say nowadays—fatalism for dummies. She is the smart kid, the self-sufficient, the slacker, the adventurer. Take her piecemeal, take her whole. *Her* life flashes across my eyes. Diapers, pacifiers, Barbies of various colors, ballet slippers, tutus, and what else do I know of her, really?

The spinning wheel slows, slows, stops, and the ball slips over a bump into the gully that belongs to the next number. Natasha laughs. "That's all."

"You'll have a story to tell the kids," I say, since it is my mission to lower the temperature.

"How—" Melanie is trying to eke out the words that have piled up inside her, but they're stuck.

"I just did," Natasha says. "I just did it. It's just what I did."

"How could you be so *stupid*?" Melanie erupts from the sofa. A split second later she jumps up and makes a dash for the bathroom.

"Don't say it," Natasha says flatly. "I know she loves me."

When Melanie comes back she is dabbing at her eyes with a tissue.

"I know, I know," Natasha says, "I was moronic."

"You would be horrified," Melanie says, "if you were sitting where I'm sitting. You would be *freaked out.*"

"Probably yes, I would be freaked out."

All our silences cluster for another exchange and reconnoiter. There is as much deep breathing as in a doctor's examining room.

Then the woman who gave birth to Natasha not quite nineteen years ago and is now, not for the first time, flooded with disbelief at what has become of her daughter shudders, flings her arms in the air, shoots her a fiery look, and declares, "I give up."

It takes a lot of hand-holding, assurances, silent recriminations, and tears before she follows up with: "I don't know why I'm being tested."

¤ ¤ ¤

AFTERWARD, MY FEELINGS spill all over each other. Relief is in the foreground but doesn't stay there for long before anger pumps in, and—what took it so long?—the insinuating, long-drawn-out whisper of guilt.

In bed, Melanie stares at the ceiling.

"I don't know how this happened," I say into the silence, "but it's not your doing. It's her doing."

"I don't care if it's the oldest cliché in the book. What did I do wrong?"

⌑⌑⌑

December 13

Two weeks have passed since the conclusion of R–CHOP, Act I, and a blood test shows that my white cells are showing signs of recovery, so it's time to blast them with R–CHOP, Act II.

The perversity of chemo: I look forward to the impending damage. It's not exactly the exhilaration of heading into battle. It's the Nietzschean exhilaration of anticipating an injury that will be good for me.

Out on Broadway, Natasha holds the taxi door open for me as if I were an old guy who needed solicitude. (In fact, I *am* an old guy who needs solicitude.) Since telling her story, she's unmistakably more chipper. She doesn't lounge around the apartment so much. Now that we're on our way to the hospital, though, she doesn't know what to say, and neither do I. I'm sure she would rather be plugged into her MP3 player, which I saw her tuck into the inner pocket of her perfectly scuffed-up leather jacket. I tell her I can take care of myself, I know the way to the hospital, I have a copy of Nietzsche's *Gay Science* for company, but in truth I'm grateful that she's coming along since, in her newly unburdened state, she is a lot more pleasant to be around, and Melanie is entitled to spend her morning in awe at a David Smith show, thinking about how well those constructions of steel manage without consciousness.

¤¤¤

When I'm done with the treatment, and the back of my hand is bandaged, Natasha helps me into a cab—gently, as if I were a paper bag with a damp bottom. As soon as we walk into the apartment, I go to the kitchen, locate the scissors, and snip off the plastic wristband with my left hand.

¤¤¤

Again, the shots in my increasingly hairless thigh. Some experiences do not lend themselves to aphorisms.

¤¤¤

I read about a study: Unhealthy people are not any less happy than healthy people.

There is no correct way to weather cancer, as there is no uniform method for love or teaching or parenthood. You live each of them in your way. Each works you over. Like a Chinese emperor with his invaluable scrolls, you stamp them with your singular mark.

⌑⌑⌑

I WEAKEN AGAIN. I drag myself down to the street most days and envy the passersby: the agreeable-looking, the plain-looking, the disagreeable-looking, the nostalgic or sullen or defiant or confident ones still wearing their Kerry/Edwards buttons, the young black women pushing white babies, the middle-aged white women pushing strollers built for twins, the white men with white stubble pushing Chinese babies. Some have cancer, and of these, some know it.

I mention the political buttons at dinner.

"Enough already about the election. You're obsessed," Melanie says.

"Wouldn't Nietzsche tell you to live in the moment?" Natasha says.

There are times when I have no idea what Nietzsche would tell me.

⌑⌑⌑

THE TEMPTATION TO congratulate oneself for being a scout—an early acquirer, as they say of technology buffs. To gain a moral advantage from being ill. There is no misfortune that cannot be turned into snobbery.

⌑⌑⌑

A DISCOVERY: I'M not bored. It takes energy to be bored.

¤¤¤

I CAN SO get satisfaction. Existing.

¤¤¤

EVEN A SICK day is a day in a life, incomplete, promising, dripping with potential. And everyone needs at least one alter ego to tend to the human spillover. I will call mine Phil and will proceed to hook him up with his own alter ego, Sophie, in a Dialogue Concerning Human Misunderstanding, to wit:

> Phil: "I realized many years ago that I wasn't in this game for the truth but the fun. An argument is a sensual thing for me. A proper syllogism is jasmine borne on the night air of the tropics. A mathematical proof is Bach's Concerto for Four Harpsichords and Strings. Gödel's theorem is Handel's Messiah. A bad so-called proof of the existence of God is rotten eggs."
>
> Sophie: "So it's all pleasure/pain. You'd rather have sex than walk on broken glass."
>
> Phil: "I'm no dope."

Sophie: "But isn't this a rather primitive way of dividing up experience? What if an argument leaves you cold?"

Phil: "I try to find something warmer."

Sophie: "Come on."

Phil: "No, really."

Sophie: "I'm trying not to be shocked. You're telling me you're indifferent to the truth?"

Phil: "Truth. After all we've been through? Aren't you getting a little long in the tooth for such innocence?"

Sophie: "Blah, blah. Let's just call it a likeness of truth, or truthlikeness, or good-enough truth, whatever you want—a statement about what we can agree is deep and enduring or—"

Phil: "You're getting cold. I'm not indifferent, exactly. If I were completely indifferent to the truth, it would mean that my moral sense and my sensual senses would have withered up and died. A spurious syllogism stinks in my nostrils, so I reject it."

Sophie: "Oh, I see. Your aesthetic sense is foolproof."

Phil: "Not hardly."

Sophie: "Your smile reminds me of a bitter lemon. If you're putting me on, you've been faking it all your professional life."

Phil: "Doesn't everybody?"

Sophie: "Now I'm going to be seriously shocked. . . ."

Phil: "Seriously, long ago I discovered I didn't have anything original to say, so I set out to make do with jollity. But there are consolations. At times I can live in the present. It's why I accept with equanimity the prospect of taking leave from this veil of amusements. It's why I'm ready to fast-forward to my memorial service."

⌑⌑⌑

AN EXERCISE FOR my book. Nietzsche as a failed vaudeville king—*Untermensch* turned *Übermensch*. Nietzsche performs Grand Guignol wearing a mustache the size of a snowplow. This thought puts me in mind of the much-reproduced 1882 photo in which his fabulous come-hither-go-away disciple and twenty-one-year-old gal pal, Lou Salomé, waves her sad little knotted-rope whip from the back of a cart that's being drawn by Nietzsche himself (staring nearsightedly into the distance) and her other miserable would-be- or maybe-already-lover, Paul Rée, a rich boy and minor apostle of the marriage of altruism and Darwinism—a depressive optimist, in other words. The rivals pose stolidly in a Swiss photographer's studio, against the backdrop of a snowy mountaintop, in good late nineteenth-century *Bürgerlich* style. Excelsior!

In bitter historical fact, poor Fritz at that precise moment is a convalescent enjoying a day off, a man on the verge of retching. Yes, *retching*—not at what humanity is becoming, not solely, at any rate, but at what *he* has become. Nietzsche is a man for whom nausea is not just a metaphor. "What is to be feared, what has a more calamitous effect than any other calamity," he writes, "is that man should inspire not profound fear but profound *nausea*," a nausea so horrible and absolute that it drives man into the arms of a "will to nothingness," namely, nihilism. The origin of depravity, in other words, is the feeling that humanity is helplessly deflating, that we are condemned to fill up with tedium. And who is responsible for the encroaching, encompassing advent of human sterility? Is it the great monsters, the forces of evil, the killers without mercy? Or, diabolically, should we blame the few *merciful* killers? Not at all. Who is to blame? "The *sick* are man's greatest danger."

What shall a sick man do with this stunning insight? Now it is 1887. He is alone. Lou Salomé has long since followed in Mathilde Trampedach's footsteps and rejected his proposal of marriage. He concludes: That brilliant creature who once made his pulse race, she is sick herself! Sickness is the rule, not the exception! He rubs his mustache. It is all too much to bear. He rushes off to the toilet. He empties himself. He gasps for breath. He is vile, a weakling, a walking stench. He gags on his own fear—his negative Eucharist. He stares into the putrid hole that is the only pilgrimage place he knows. His knees weaken. He is sick unto death of his rotten mind. He takes deep breaths until he can stand upright without fear of the next convulsion. He pours himself a glass of water and drains it, though he knows it will only hasten him back to the toilet. He staggers back to his sitting room, feeling his way from doorknob to bureau, then throws himself back on his pillow before his legs have a chance to give way. He rubs his mustache again and then—Here it is! The sick man invents the absolute health that comes from learning to love your fate! *Amor fati*, he writes in 1888, his last sane year.

The fools, and worse, who later claimed Nietzsche as a high-intensity priest, like Freud or, in his own way, the ultimate monster, Adolf Hitler (who could not have actually read, let alone understood, more than a lurid sentence or two, but never mind), failed to see how badly the battered Friedrich was ruled by his fear of enervation.

"Everywhere"—that is his word, *everywhere*—Nietzsche sees "the struggle of the sick against the healthy. . . . That the sick should not make the healthy sick—and this is what such an emasculation would involve—should surely be our supreme concern on earth; but this requires above all that the healthy should be *segregated* from the sick, guarded even from the sight of the sick, that they may not confound themselves with the sick."

Nietzsche was certainly no Jew-hater—"I am just having all anti-Semites shot," he wrote to his oldest friend in one of his last letters (signed "Dionysus")—but isn't it plain that he was on the side of quarantine if not concentration camps? He thought there was such a thing as "life unworthy of life." We who love Nietzsche, what do we do with such a phrase? Shall we get him off the hook—partway off—by reading between his lines to see how intensely he was projecting? He climbed to the summit of his self-loathing, where he perched, poised to jump, for years, until finally he went over the edge.

Au contraire, I want nothing more than to rejoin the healthy. "A wise person moves among people like a botanist around plants," Nietzsche wrote, but I have not arrived at that kind of detachment. Despite my better judgment, I don't just study people, I am capable of liking them after all, though I can hear the objection Melanie would have raised even before my body went bad on me: "You go on about humanity, but at this particular moment in this particular apartment my segment of humanity would like to request of your segment of humanity that you clean off the table and wash the wineglasses thoroughly enough so that I don't have to wash them again." I do like life among human animals. I like their ruddy looks, their air of being accompanied even in solitude, the intense way they rush through the frigid streets lugging their plastic shopping bags on the way back to their overheated apartments. I feel tenderly toward them with their cell phone conversations about real estate, their infantile humor, their scowls, their intense self-involvement, their humorless gripes, their politeness and aimless aggression, their sagging eyelids, their refusal to give up their seats for pregnant women, their facial surgery. I bask among them. Even as I scorn them, they invigorate me.

It's not true that in my sick heart of hearts, I want to bring them down.

Perhaps I'll call my book *Triumph of the Ill.*

¤¤¤

NIETZSCHE NEVER HAD to cope with a sick child, or an errant child, or even a conventionally rambunctious one. Even his loathsome sister failed to reproduce, so he was never conscripted to babysit. He never had to comfort a whimpering infant, or one with a hacking cough, or a high fever, or diarrhea, and wonder what to do. He never changed a diaper, or worried if he had hired the right person to do that, or had to contend with a wife awakened at three in the morning to breast-feed. He was never depended upon by someone abjectly dependent. He never had to ask himself if he was reliable. He never feared for the health of his baby's tiny lungs. He never sat in a doctor's waiting room holding his squalling flesh and blood. He never tried to comfort his inconsolable child awakened in the middle of the night and unable, for once, to say where she hurt, and to wait for the pediatrician to deliver the news that this sounds like night terrors, and there is no telling when they will repeat. He never forced the little one to swallow a pill, or bundled a baby up and dashed across town to sit for hours in an emergency room pretending to be patient or agonizing about whether he was too much so. He never pretended to decipher baby talk. He never scourged himself for making the wrong decision. He never saw the human line replenish itself, learn, fail, and replenish itself again. The desert of time held no oases for him. What does Zarathustra have to say to an anxious parent?

If a parent is lucky, his child is only sick once in a while. But even a healthy child is a nuisance. She throws tantrums. She throws food. She drools on the furniture. She picks indefinable scraps up off the floor and sticks them into her mouth. She is whimsical and incomprehensible. Then she becomes comprehensible the way an antagonist becomes comprehensible. Even a daughter, supposedly more docile, contends with her father. My own daughter always knew her own mind. The daughter demands, the father commands, the daughter rebels, the father defends and from time to time learns. A man who does not contend with his child will remain—eternally—the younger generation. His sullenness is the sullenness of a child. His rejection of the past and contempt for the future, his life in the eternal present, are those of a child. His triumphal flourishes are gestures of "Look, Ma, no hands." His indifference, audacity, aloofness, foolishness, rebellion, brilliance, and show-offishness are all those of a child.

Look at me. Look at Nietzsche, who—after the death of his little brother—will remain for the rest of his days the lone little colossus-son of his mother's life.

Poor solitary, grandiose Nietzsche! Because no one will need him, or challenge him, he is reduced to wrestling with himself. Because no one strives to overcome him, he gives birth to himself as the avatar of self-overcoming. In the guise of Zarathustra, he impersonates a god. He rants against "the most contemptible thing," that pathetic, health-obsessed creature he calls "the last man"—a man without offspring! He is that most despicable man equal to every other despicable man! Blinking and gullible, puffed up, never inventing, never honorable, bitterly envious of all whose ideas and inventions he relies on, too cowardly to distrust everything in the universe that deserves distrust, this weak, gray creature crows that he needs neither the pleasure of power nor the pleasure of obedience, that he is unburdened by such risky ambitions, that he has discovered true happiness because . . . he needs comfort, convenience, security . . . and therefore he will agree to love his pathetic neighbor, that feeble thing, as himself!

So the king of the hill rants and raves against this sterile "last man"—himself.

¤ ¤ ¤

My beard is looking patchy. My pubic hair is starting to go. Infancy, here we come.

I weigh myself obsessively every morning. I was around 190 when this started. I've just passed 180, heading downward, though my appetite has returned and I'm scarfing down chocolate bars. I insist on treating my loss of weight as an achievement. The pathetic mental calisthenics of the Americans!

¤ ¤ ¤

Natasha appears for dinner completely bald. Melanie gasps and bursts into tears. I'm frozen, the way Natasha used to be as an infant when she was startled (once, by a little angel of death who showed up at the door on Halloween, another time by a peacock fanning his tail at the zoo). My eyes water. Then I jump up, go to her, throw my arms around her neck, as Nietzsche is supposed to have done to a horse who was being beaten—his last act before he went over the brink into absolute madness. (He may have gotten the idea from *Crime and Punishment*, so I can get the idea from him.)

"You shouldn't have."

"Hey, I should have. I've been meaning to. It's no big deal."

"It's a very big deal," I say, "and I'm really touched."

Even in infancy, she sported a tiny little mop of hair. I know how much her hair means to her. It's her trophy, even her pet. But perhaps in her circle the egg-dome is considered an attractive look if your head is ovular, which hers is.

Not least, she's made a decision about herself.

"By the way," says her mother, "the shape of your head is very attractive."

"It brings out your eyes," I say.

"OK, guys, enough!" she says.

¤ ¤ ¤

OUT FOR A walk, I step deliberately, and Melanie slows to keep pace with me so my eyes can keep company with my feet. New York wants you to earn your right to stroll safely. Arm in arm like Victorians who barely know how to have a good time, we amble to the edge of Riverside Park. A blessing, a tease of nature, even when the trees are winter bare. When I remember to pay attention, I live a glorious life. When I look down, I see gouges and indentations. I behold mysteries. *Behold* originally meant: to keep.

No matter how creamy, nothing keeps. Time, right now, is the element in which we imagine the timeless.

¤ ¤ ¤

December 21

I've been meaning to call my old friend Jack Newfield, who was diagnosed with cancer just before I was. "Meaning to call" means that my impulse to call him was canceled out by my clumsiness whenever I tried to imagine the conversation. Cancer talk has lost its novelty. So I didn't call. Inquisitive Jack, who loved to track down slum landlords and crooked nursing homes, and to gossip about backroom political deals. Fearless Jack, who didn't care what some infantile leftist would think of his calling Fidel Castro a dictator. His knowing look, as if he were peering through you, or down at you from the corner of the ceiling. We ran into each other, with our wives, on the street—was it September 13 or 14, 2001?—and went out for dinner next to the little improvised shrine of candles and flowers that materialized in front of the local fire station—telling the stories New Yorkers told in those days, retelling the ones we'd already told and the ones we'd just heard, assuring ourselves that we were alive and still sentient, anything to establish that the calamity of the pulverized towers right down the street had *happened* and we were here to talk about it.

Jack had something much worse than lymphoma: kidney cancer, spread to his lung. Now the news comes: He died last night.

Now I can (barely) begin to imagine how a final conversation might have gone. He says he's curious about dying. I say I've discovered I'm not afraid to die. He says that death doesn't interest him but dying does. I say that Nietzsche was right: The human problem is not death, but life.

Chat with a dead man: the afterglow.

⌑⌑⌑

NATASHA IS READING Agatha Christie again. I've run out of conversational gambits except for occasional comments on the stubble cropping up on her skull, which I pet once in a while.

⌑⌑⌑

December 28

Susan Sontag dead, her second recurrence of cancer, terminal this time. Topics I would love to have discussed with her: chemotherapy as metaphor, libido after cancer, Nietzsche and insecurity. Would she have torn into my new book, insisting that just as illness is not a metaphor, it cannot be the starting point for a philosophy, not consciously, not even unconsciously; that illness is just illness, just a disorder of cells, all the way down? I suspect she would have disapproved of my latest project, with an incandescent smile and a toss of her royal head. If she was consistent at all, which she wasn't always, except that she was equally adamant every time she arrived at a position. But the complicated pain I feel, reading her obit, starts with the recognition that her death—for me—marks another failure of mine, an incompletion.

We crossed paths many times during the '80s. When we were introduced in Berkeley, where I lived then, she said, "Oh, I read everything you write." She gave me her phone number in New York and told me to keep calling, since she answered the phone every other time it rang and didn't have an answering machine. For a few years, I did call. We were friends, even. I admired her criticizing the *Nation* in public for having less to say about the Soviet Union than *Reader's Digest*. She supported me for a fellowship. We went to a club called Interferon that I was told authoritatively was a Mafia laundry. I told her once that I had nominated her for a fellowship that would bring her to Berkeley for a semester. Her reaction: "Why would I want to do that?" (The academics, for their part, wanted her curriculum vitae and an extended letter of nomination from me; I didn't bother.)

Over the next few years, I went on calling her when I got to New York. She liked to gossip: about A.'s wife with her multiple husbands, the famous writer B. as an alcoholic, the poet C. who thought the sloppy novelist D. was a superior writer because he *loved* D.—the word *love* filled her throat like honey, and I felt as if I had been granted a privileged peephole into the universe of love. She liked to chortle over the nincompoops she met at outlying campuses where she lectured. She called Maui, where her sister lived, "the asshole of the universe." I lapped it all up. She spoke of her comings and goings in the tone of reviewing her own court performances.

Her enemies called her aloof. It wasn't always so. She was kind when I told her my girlfriend Jane had cancer. Strangers stared at her in the diner as we talked about the recurrence studies conducted by a doctor in Milan. She told me she was in therapy to find out why it was hard for her to feel. I didn't know what to say.

A few times we walked to Chinatown for dim sum. With her long legs, she strode. Once a truck came barreling down on us as we crossed Canal Street. I grabbed her hand, and fancied I'd saved her life—tabloid headline material.

Then I was back in New York once, and called her about getting together. She said she was revising a story for the *New Yorker* and hadn't the time to see me. A short story, not some piece of time-bound journalism. Why couldn't it wait? The last time I ran into her in Berkeley, after she gave a reading. We ended up at dinner together at Chez Panisse, but she brought along the haughty climber Caroline, who's making a career as a professional insider and sneers at me, though not at me alone. Susan declined to take up *my* invitations to call when she was visiting the Bay Area. So I stopped calling.

Deep down, I came to suspect, she was contemptuous of my unbridled moralism—a trait in myself I was actually trying to dismantle with Nietzsche's help. In Stephen Spender's journals from the '60s there is a note on her disdain for moralists. When I read that, I felt a quiver of recognition—she must have seen me as a rube.

My, such a jealous and insecure lover, Alan! How much of this harshness is envy, which is ever and always disfigurement? Who am I to chastise Susan Sontag for inconsistency? If I am less conspicuously so, it might be only because I'm stodgier, or more polite.

She was a seductive queen; I was not her true prince, and resented it. Seduced and abandoned. Unrequited intellectual love—my weakness.

The last time I saw her, maybe a year ago, was at a meeting about Iraq.

Afterward, we had cocktails. She was cool, but the last thing she said to me was, "Great to see you." As Sartre wrote, what you never know about another person is his or her sincerity.

The world is piling up with corpses. My world.

¤ ¤ ¤

WHAT KIND OF a man feels sorry for himself after a tsunami sweeps people away and obliterates villages all around the Indian Ocean?

Stalin, perceptive social scientist that he was, worked it out: A million deaths are a statistic.

¤ ¤ ¤

DO I SERIOUSLY imagine I can think my way into the mind of a severely impaired itinerant German genius and would-be demigod born a full century before me, a cosmopolitan who never set foot in the United States, who possibly never made love to a woman whom he didn't pay for the privilege, who never drove an auto or saw a movie or heard of a world war or the atomic bomb? I flatter myself!

I think many things would become clear to me, seriously, if I could visit another consciousness for a while, just drop in and poke around for an hour, lift up each feeling for a minute or two, fondle it, turn it around, then return it delicately to its shelf. Then I might begin to know what the continuity of the universe feels like.

The philosophy of consciousness is rich with ways to disguise our ineptitude.

¤ ¤ ¤

ANOTHER DANK DAY, the sky groaning under the weight of what pilots call a low ceiling. Winter creeps into the bones. Faces look ravaged. Brick facades disappear behind wooden scaffolds. The city could use a coat of snow. Still, the sidewalk keeps rewarding my close attention. I'm struck by the casual way in which people discard trash, and the trash then turns into an aesthetic object if you learn to see it the right way, like a cardboard milk shake cup in the middle of the sidewalk, passersby going out of their way to avoid it. It's as if the world is cracking a joke. An analogue to what Nietzsche said: "People who think deeply feel themselves to be comedians in their relationship with others because they first have to simulate a surface in order to be understood." Like Susan. The discarded cup on a Broadway sidewalk reveals the world's inner experience. The cup and sidewalk are layers of skin, "which reveals something but *conceals* even more."

I'm tripping out. The world doesn't speak in a single voice, so "it" cannot crack a joke. The world is cacophony. Or rather, the world does not sit still to *be* anything at all. *Being* is what we yearn to know when we don't understand that there is no joke to get. Sometimes a discarded cup is just a discarded cup.

⌑ ⌑ ⌑

I FANCY THAT I know exactly what Nietzsche means by "simulating a surface." Possibly it starts the day your parents teach you to respond to a gift by saying *Thank you.* You catch on. You see that it pleases them when you speak the magic words. You have become comprehensible—apparently. The audience coos with delight.

So do you learn, too, to "have" a self, "that within which passeth show"? And who is it, really, who stands "within"? Is this interior self, this homunculus, anything but an artifact of grammar, because Indo-European languages resort to the first person? Is the self, deep down, shallow—itself a mask, always extruding new layers, like (dare I say it?) a tumor? Persona, appearance, mask. The guises you need to reveal yourself—your *something*.

Reveal or repeal?

⌑ ⌑ ⌑

THE DISCONCERTING DOUBLENESS of the ill.

"You sound fine," people say to me.

Meaning, I suppose, *You don't wheeze, moan, or cough, your voice doesn't tremble, you aren't hoarse, you don't sound feeble, you sound like—yourself?*

Yes, that's how I sound.

I've learned to make small talk, reacting to *How are you?* without descending to *Fine*, instead playing with *Not so bad*, *Getting by*, *Managing*, *Could be worse*, *Maintaining*, *Nice weather we're having*. In truth, I'm tempted to say, *Why do you ask? Why should you care?* But Melanie is right when she says, "It won't kill you to be polite." Drive-by mordancy is a cheap all-purpose pose. What do I have to lose by trying on the trappings and the suits of gentleness, even optimism, given that you never know enough to justify holding either a benign view of human intentions or the opposite?

As intently as I listen, my lymph system gives up no evidence, no signal, no mutter, no clue of its inner life, nothing. I can't tell whether my lymphatic cells have resumed their proper equilibrium or gone awry again. What I notice is that I'm no longer losing weight. I eat with relish. I consume but am not consumed. Eating is like sex, but easier. My pubic hair continues to thin out, as does the hair on my chest, arms, legs. I'm losing my primate nature along with my animal passion. Does this mean that I'm regressing to infancy or passing to the dark side of old age?

I don't know. If you want to know how I am, *ignorant* is the answer. But if people call and ask how you are and you say, *I don't know*, they think you're rude.

For years I've preached a certain respect for indeterminacy as an ethical commitment. The quest for certainty leads over a cliff. First came religious certainty, then philosophical, political, and scientific certainty, and each led to catastrophe. Religious certainty was invidious, leading to endless war against objectors who groaned under the weight of their own certainties. Philosophical certainty canceled out beautiful, flawed reality: Nietzsche was dead right to revolt against the Platonic rejection of life, which led to the Hebraic rejection, which led to the Christian rejection, *und so weiter*. Now, love of mystery has become my second nature. It's like a hammock, suspending me and blocking the hunger to know the destiny of those hitherto undistinguished cells running amok—cells with no will, no intention, no consciousness, blind, deaf, and dumb cells, killer cells, mechanical and impersonal cells, yet with no indeterminacy about their effects.

And so I must ask, in all innocence: In what sense are those murderous cells "mine"? And I must answer, in all honesty: They are no less so than my fingernails. I might renounce the cancerous cells, but they don't renounce me.

Idea for an article: "Negative Narcissism: The Body as an Embarrassment." Or, "Fast Food, Class Fate, and the Weight of the Cross." To look in the mirror and feel revolted—the post-postmodern experience. To sneak one look after another because you happen to be passing a plate-glass window . . . just because the image is right there and you must—because you *can*—get updates on the look of your sack of flesh. Because you are visible.

"The body" is all the rage among my colleagues—a long-overdue recoil against Descartes. But it must also be a consequence of the fact that in their actual lives they're chained to their laptops for hours every day, and perhaps also because they live in a state of advancing decay or they can smell it coming—an odor of the mortal animal beginning to die. Unhealthy minds in unhealthy bodies, they go to the gym to *work out*, to *work up a sweat*. Their abs are their answers to the perennial question of academics, *What are you working on?* We exercise to turn ourselves into fitness machines. No wonder growing old shames us.

I can see the crowds packing the ballroom for an MLA session on, say, "The Burden of the Body." In this fantasy, I wear a sharp yellow tie with my sleekest Italian suit, the red-tinged rust job with the pale stripes. I take the stage smiling craftily. The wrinkles fanning out from my eyes signal a powerful magnetic field. Women wonder what it would be like to conference-fuck me. I seem to *get* them.

In fact, my beautifully tailored, just-loose-enough-looking suit is the proof that I don't actually hate my body, or fear it, nor do I fear blowing the whistle on everyone else who does fear the withering, sagging, and bulging of their flesh. I win points for fearlessness and tailoring, as if the second is really the first—a mistake many people make.

From the moment I open my mouth I can taste the post-session apple martini in the hotel bar with the assistant professor who arrived early to sit in the front row, the one with the impossibly big brown eyes, yes, that one, she whom all eyes of all sexes undress. . . . She sips her Cosmopolitan and talks about her forthcoming paper on the construction of cosmopolitanism and I simulate interest.

⌑ ⌑ ⌑

IN THE MIDST of chemotherapy, my fantasy life takes this turn. It figures.

⌑ ⌑ ⌑

AFTERTHOUGHT ON AN unsolved problem in evolutionary theory: How does the propensity for malignant tumors work to my advantage? Or Natasha's, or her descendants', or that of the species at large? What does the mayhem of cancer do for the relative longevity of my genes? Since cancer is largely a disease of the old, does it benefit the middle-aged to lose their parents, and does that, in turn, benefit the young? (But if there's a genetic component in cancer and the answers are yes and yes, why don't the young who come down with cancer die out once and for all?) And if cancer confers no advantage in the struggle for existence, if it confers an evident disadvantage, in fact, but still has a genetic base, why did it evolve in the first place? For what silver lining is it the cloud?

¤ ¤ ¤

READING THE PAPERS as an emetic. The sampling of reality as a reason to make a man retch. Nietzsche in *The Gay Science* (make that *Joyful Knowledge*):

> One thinks with a watch in one's hand, even as one eats one's midday meal while reading the latest news of the stock market; one lives as if one might "miss out on something."

The thought of Nietzsche holding the newspaper up to his feeble eyes to check the stocks in the first place—a hoot.

Or think of Nietzsche contemplating America's personification of handsome incomprehension and clueless vigor, our triumph of will over judgment. The emergence of George W. Bush as the chief powerhouse of humanity is a tribute to the fecklessness of the privileged, the breakdown of a worthy aristocracy in favor of bullshit artists—

But hold on a minute. Doesn't the ascendancy of George W. Bush pose a devastating test for Nietzsche? Doesn't Bush pass the vitality test? Isn't his will-not-to-know, or at least willingness-not-to-know, the foundation of his power? Isn't he the champion of impulsiveness, the proof that reason can once and for all be overcome? George Bush, meet Friedrich Nietzsche; Friedrich Nietzsche, meet George Bush. I turn this encounter over to our host:

> —*Mr. Bush, you have already said that Jesus is your favorite philosopher. I have a follow-up line of questioning for Mr. Nietzsche. If everyone is in the grip of a will to power and Mr. Bush here is the guy who forced his way up front, then who is to say that he is not a fitting master? He acquired hordes of marching morons to sing his praises, so how unworthy can he be? Has he not achieved that fullness of self-realization of which you speak? You speak of self-overcoming, he speaks of being born again, but are the two of you really speaking of anything different? Sir?*

¤¤¤

THE PROTESTATION OF innocence is the most detestable of all-too-human traits. A Nietzschean overman would never stoop so low as to blame everyone else in sight and proclaim his unique and utter innocence. He would own up to his ignorance. Innocence is an undersupply of awareness. There's nobody here but us fools.

¤¤¤

In honor of Susan Sontag, I resolve to resist speaking of a metastasis of evil.

¤ ¤ ¤

But let's pause for a moment to revisit the chronic problem of evil. One possible approach: God was so weakened by the effort of the Creation, which brought time into the world, that when He was done, His powers spent, the Devil crept into the universe. The Devil was a remnant, an outsider, who took advantage of time to recover—like the Terminator being blown to bits but reviving, collecting himself, scooping himself back into shape. So God once stood outside time, but when the world fell into time, He lost his omnipotence. He was a *failed* God—and therein lay his majesty, because He could not bear to be responsible for having created a world that fell so far short of the good.

Yet it was good.

¤ ¤ ¤

After class, I go to the men's room, look in the mirror, see that my cheek is going red—a rash—suppose that I'm dying. . . .

Try not to think about lymphoma.

¤ ¤ ¤

Natasha moping around. Through the door to my study, one afternoon, I hear Melanie say to her: "You know, your grim face is not the best thing for morale around here."

The sound of a big sob comes from my daughter.

¤ ¤ ¤

My colleague Mark's young, beautiful wife, a poet about to publish her first book, mother of their baby boy, went to the gym, got on the exercise bicycle, blacked out, and never recovered. She suffered from a heart arrhythmia. Mark is sitting shiva. People mill around helplessly. The baby is blissful. The words *I don't know what to say* were made for this occasion. What would Nietzsche say?

¤ ¤ ¤

Happy New Year. Melanie and I stay home. Natasha goes out with her friends. I make no resolutions. I miss champagne. A man who needn't make resolutions is a happy man.

¤ ¤ ¤

January 2, 2005

Natasha back on the living room sofa at all hours.

Melanie doesn't seem to know what to say to her either. So we're all just there, coexisting.

Try not to think about the upcoming scans. The dinner table is piled high with avoidance.

¤¤¤

January 18

Moments of truth. This is the day of the CAT scan to see whether the R–CHOP treatments have succeeded in wiping out the cancer—*my* cancer.

I sit in the waiting room; drink the banana-flavored elixir, metallic but less chemical-tasting this time; wait and wait. On the other side of the room sits a rotund ultra-Orthodox Jewish man who accompanies his thirteen-year-old daughter in braces. He tries to convince her to accept an IV needle. She is pale with fear. His voice is soft, patient.

Eventually my name is called. I am escorted into a dressing room. I take off my shirt, put on a gown. When I return to the waiting room to drink my second container of fluid, the gigantic man in the yarmulke is gently trying to persuade his daughter that the needle won't hurt her.

Then my name is called and I'm ushered into a frigid room and slotted into the torus-shaped machine, a cold womb. An IV is stuck in my arm, and I fill up with a warm metallic feeling. The attendant stands by impassively and watches me slide into the machine. My face almost grazes the metal tube.

Tomorrow, the PET scan will survey my body with a different technique. PET stands for "positron emission tomography."

While the CAT discerns structures (what the body is made of), the PET discerns functional processes (what the body is doing). If I pass the PET, we proceed to the second phase of chemo. If I flunk, more-strenuous treatments will follow—stem cell injections, transplants, and whatnot—but even then, all is not lost. Not all.

Hold that thought.

⌑ ⌑ ⌑

January 21

My scan results from Josie, Dr. Berg's nurse, over the phone:

"Preliminary results. PET: There's been a resolution of areas and no new areas. CAT shows moderate to marked improvement. Presumably this means the tumors are 'no longer viable.' The lymph nodes that were bulging have decreased. The doctor is very pleased."

Very *pleased*. *Very* pleased. Josie is a straight arrow. She may be reading from a script but she does so with utmost sincerity. I believe her. Relief wells up inside, a palpable sensation that starts in my depths and rolls upward into the place where my tears are stored. When my doctor is very pleased, I am very pleased.

Of course, not being the sort to indulge in premature celebrations, I have to ask what "moderate to marked" means. It means there are no longer tumors growing, but there are remnants—tumors that were zapped but left husks behind. Husks are innocuous.

I fill my lungs, and exuberance pours through me, a sweetness of gratitude, a whole swelling relief, and the world turns—why not say it straight out?—glorious.

So my luck is back, even if it has an odd way of revealing itself. Even if it means that as soon as the weekend is over I will drag myself back to the hospital for Phase II, which will entail three-day, two-night stays for slow infusions of the chemical cocktail ICE that is supposed to prevent the revival of a malignancy stemming from any murderous cells left unscrubbed by the first phase. There are to be three of these rounds, at two-week intervals. If my blood counts are good enough and I don't catch cold, or worse, in the interim. In that case, we delay.

I line up guest speakers for the two classes I'll miss, on the Federalist Papers and Rousseau, respectively. And I make a reservation for Melanie and me at the best restaurant on the Upper West Side, for ten days after the date of my first "discharge"—as if I were due for an ejaculation, or the hospital were a gun and the patient a bullet. By then I should be getting up the strength to submit to the next round of ICE.

In class, when I announce the forthcoming substitutes, one distinctly perceptive or at least forthright student asks in a squeaky voice, "Are you all right?"

My God, they have been watching me wither all these weeks. I'm touched that somebody notices. Even better, it is one of my favorite students. “I’m fine,” I say, smiling and meaning it.

Fine sounds better than *reprieved. Fine* refers to a present tense that in principle might go on indefinitely. *Reprieved* is stamped with an expiration date, even if a blurred one. I like the ring of *fine*.

⌑ ⌑ ⌑

FINE, THEN. I have a blank weekend to ready myself. Be practical about reading matter: Will I want Tolstoy in the hospital? Raymond Chandler? Back issues of the *New York Review of Books*? What about Nietzsche? Without question I’ll keep up with the course reading, even if next week is Kant Week. When I was being relieved of my inflamed appendix, aged twenty-two, two of my college buddies brought me a book of fairly discreet pornography called something like *Confessions of a French Maid*—I recall the squarish pages, the line drawings of curves and short skirts. But perhaps the mood this time will not be so hard to arrange, although I am less limber or, to put it mildly, less easily aroused.

Filling the emptiness of time. Indeed, my head is not roomy enough to live in. I always start with the same deck but each day affords a chance to shuffle my feelings around and reconnoiter. Notes toward a mood: In a month, I’ll be done with this whole—what shall we call it?—interlude, adventure, crash course in the nature of things.

In the course of the morning the Hudson passes from a continuous bright cerulean to a heavier blue discolored by a large block of green that breaks into distinct bands. The river, shadowed by clouds, churns down to the sea, carrying batches of whitecaps, and the sea doesn't go anywhere, it simply is. The cold light crashes against the bright white brick apartment building across Broadway, illuminating an American flag affixed to the top floor of the fire escape, rippling mildly, signaling something that endures ("the flag was still there"), for better and worse.

Howie, one of my college buddies who was so good as to bring me *Confessions of a French Maid*, good Howie, who succeeded in "going all the way" with the beautiful Wendy when I couldn't get to second base, and later left me a note asking me to come to his room because he wanted to apologize (so this is what real life is like, I remember thinking)—Howie died not long ago of a very virulent cancer.

I sputter, but I'm alive.

¤ ¤ ¤

Saturday, January 22

The Knicks having lost nine out of their last ten games, most recently after giving up their last possession without being able to get off a shot in twenty-four seconds and then watching the Houston Rockets score at the buzzer, Lenny Wilkens resigns as coach.

Basketball is not like life. It's more like Greek tragedy, which is born, as Nietzsche taught us, in music, this time with a dying fall. Cue wah-wah trumpet.

¤ ¤ ¤

When I emerge from the TV room after the dismal Houston game, Melanie and Natasha are embracing next to the dining room table and Melanie is saying: "If this is what you want."

"What did I miss?"

"Tell him," Natasha says.

"I think you should tell him."

My daughter looks at me, red-eyed, oscillating before my eyes between teenager and woman, and says, "I waited until we found out that you're going to be OK, and now I want you to know that I'm pregnant."

Melanie recounts later, in the bedroom, that when the two of them were alone Natasha added: "I'm not going to have another abortion. I can't go through that again—" That's when she burst into tears, and that's when Melanie got up and hugged her.

She was stunned, Melanie told me. Stunned numb. Thinking: This is a soap opera saga—drop out of school, run around with a drug gang, have an abortion or abortions, get pregnant.

The father is a guy Natasha met in a bar on election night. About him, Natasha has little to say—and the fact that she has little to say is the news. Melanie doesn't press. I follow her lead.

She's due in August.

I'll be sticking around for a while, and now I know what I'll be sticking around to see, and what do I care how pat this might seem? The little girl of mine who once had astoundingly blonde hair, she who insisted on wearing a dress whether she was walking in the woods or going to a birthday party, she who with impulsive and extravagant delight ignited the room when she toddled to the window for no other purpose than to watch the birds, she is now herself a bringer of life, taking her place in the endless line of human reprieves. There will be troubles along the way, for she seems barely able to take care of herself, let alone a child. There is the problem of the mysteriously absent father, and the problem of making a living. But I don't object to a spurt of sentimentality about life going on from reprieve to reprieve, that is, from generation to generation. Generation, generate, generous—the etymology is proof that we replenish ourselves and so the human race throws itself into time immemorial and unending—

Beget, by God, be God, begin the beguine—

Joy floods the room, joy in my bones, reckless joy, joy of the blood, joy of the heart, joy circulating to places beyond my probably healthy lymph.

¤ ¤ ¤

NATASHA SLEEPS TILL after eleven. I tell her gingerly that I don't want to press but if there's anything she wants to tell me about the father of her child, I'm listening. She says thanks, she's still trying to think this through. Then I ask if she's absolutely made up her mind about having the child.

"Absolutely. A closed question. It's not a question."

That's that. I resign the pulpit.

⌑ ⌑ ⌑

Monday, January 24

But I am still a chemotherapy patient with work to do.

In the hospital lobby, I watch a very old woman bent over like an apostrophe with a cane. An even older man slogs into the elevator pushing his walker. I pull myself up to my full height.

Fluorescent light is up-to-the-minute light, institutional light, the light of efficiency, the office, the mortuary; the light that flattens dimensions, that burns away shadows; the light of persistence, birth, learning, recovery.

⌑ ⌑ ⌑

THEY DO MARVELOUS things with hospital beds these days. Not only is there one button to raise and lower the head and another to raise and lower the foot, but the surface of the bed purrs and wiggles, as if its skin were alive. I might as well be stretched out on the back of a friendly animal. The effect the first time is startling.

Banded for identification like a bird, I'm being "infused" with etoposide, the E component of the treatment called ICE. The compounds labeled I and C will come later, along with Rituxan, the R in R–CHOP. Melanie wears a mask and rubber gloves. I'm infectable. To protect me, my visitors must hide.

Now that I'm hooked up and lying inert, Melanie heads off for errands and editing. Bless her, she has a household to run and I'm not much help—in fact, I'm one of the household items requiring attention, like dirty dishes.

She leans over and kisses me goodbye. It's not exactly sexy to be kissed on the lips by a woman wearing a mask. But if you think about it the right way, it's funny. In any case, I feel about as sexy as a damp mop. Never mind. A farewell in a hospital room has a tenderness all its own.

A transparent plastic bag filled with benign poison hangs from a tall wheeled pole behind me. The stuff drips through a series of tubes into the back of my hand. A little bubble makes its way down the IV line like an ant along a wire. The toxins make their way into my bloodstream, and I stare out the window at the Queensboro Bridge, and think that all elaborate bridges are splendid, even clumsy ones, and that Nietzsche would think them splendid, too, and wonder whether he would have taken the benefits of modern medicine with grim amusement or given in, for a moment, to awe.

I try to read Kant's *Groundwork for the Metaphysics of Morals*, which I will teach on Thursday, but Kant and I have company. On the other side of the pale curtain that divides this semiprivate room—why not call it semipublic, for that matter?—the TV is clicking through multiple stations: "Doesn't that beat all get-out? To be that kind of underachiever?" "It's been a while since the Knicks looked like a .500 team." "President Bush addresses an antiabortion rally and says that he supports their cause." "I encourage you to take heart from our achievements, because a true culture of life cannot be sustained solely by changing laws. We need, most of all, to change hearts." Click. A female voice says, "You didn't tell me," punctuated by an organ note. You can spend the day flicking around the dial feeling superior, an American overman surrounded by underachievers. Eventually, an electronic voice brimming with confidence says: "The question now is how the defense is going to rebut this very effective witness."

I have been wondering what is "the question" all my life. Kant, who is no slouch, would say that the question is whether there is a basis for universal morality if God bows out. I devoutly hope there is, since the absurdities of religion are a huge price to pay before we agree to be good or even not half bad. (We should be impressed by a deity who consigns six million Jews to unimaginable torture and assembly-line slaughter because He has a plan? Suppose He's already unveiled it? Suppose we've already been assigned our roles in the horror movie?) The question posed by the brisk, barely human voice on the other side of the curtain is not a question I feel like answering, or devoting a single second to thinking about.

"She is simply an incredible witness," the voice shouts. This she means as a compliment.

Another voice, brassier, southern, comes back: "Believe you me. Ann, what about the jurors? Are they rolling their eyes? Are they snorting? You've got to be able to read something from this jury."

The reporter says something I can't make out, and the brassy voice goes rollicking: "Not gonna happen! Not gonna happen!"

I put aside Kant for *Conversations with Nietzsche*, a fun book of reminiscences by people who had the exalted experience of spending some time with the sage of revaluation and, weirdly and wonderfully, felt graced by him.

Battered old Nietzsche, flat on his back in his narrow bed under his cold compresses, was frantic enough without an electronic noise barrage. He could lie quietly, drifting down the river of his agony, taking the full measure of the miseries and occasional joys of a struggle that he exalted by calling it self-overcoming—all the while doubting whether self-overcoming was possible for him at all, or whether, even if possible, it was worth the teeth-gritting effort; fearing that no matter how hard he gritted his teeth, he was being hurled inexorably toward the abyss. He never longed for an iPod. He supplied his own internal soundtrack. He was unplugged.

I do not have the stamina for Raymond Chandler. I am not drawn to the jigsaw puzzles that the pale nurse, no advertisement for health herself, informed me are available for borrowing from the library upstairs. I stare at the ceiling, strangely at ease. I am reduced to a conduit for the elixir working its way through my blood.

"Let's face it, Carol," says the TV voice, "they weren't prepared for the DA's bold move."

"Damn right," says another voice, baritone, quiet but clear—my roommate's, from the other side of the curtain. I drift off to sleep without hearing Carol's reply. The chemo must be working because my mind has turned to a swamp.

¤ ¤ ¤

THE TRILL OF a cell phone nearby, not my own, awakens me.

"Yup," says my roommate, in a vigorous baritone. "Your voice too. . . . No, I'm fine. No, really. . . . nothing I can't manage. I'm a manager, right? . . . There's nothing I can't manage. . . . They don't know. . . . Don't worry, it's just a bump in the road. . . . Tomorrow or Thursday, I expect. . . . How's the little one? No, I wouldn't bring him. I don't want to scare him. . . . I haven't. . . . I've got Court TV to remind me of what I'm missing. . . . Hospital TV, hospital food, it's all the same. . . . Could be worse. . . . No, I'm not worried. . . . You too, honey." There's the sound of an air kiss and then he goes silent.

¤¤¤

BIZARRE, THE WAY a curtain functions as a wall and remains a curtain. How old is my roommate? How sick? How tall, how thin? Wiry, I'm guessing, with aggressive cords in his neck. His voice is soaked with authority. It's not Nietzsche's voice, which is supposed to have been so soft that sometimes his friends had to crane closer to make him out. My hearty roommate is a man who is used to being in charge. I know as little about him as about the lawyer-experts on Court TV. They might be equally sick, for all I know, though one knows it and the other does not.

Outside, the midday light is glinting brightly off the steely, uncouth Queensboro Bridge.

¤¤¤

I DOZE OFF. When I return to a semblance of consciousness, my roommate is talking again, this time straining to smooth the rough edges. "June!" with a little lilt. "I've been better. . . . There's still a lot that they don't know. . . . But probably it's a recurrence of the leukemia. My count's in the low hundreds. . . . I know." Then his voice slides up the scale, and he almost barks: "Don't worry, I'm not expiring. What do I sound like, a credit card? A milk carton? . . . I'll let you know if they give me an expiration date. . . . No. I'm not going home today. They're saying another day or two. . . . There's no telling. . . . I know, I know. . . . It'll be great to see you, too."

He's the commanding type, the kind of guy who, when he plays poker, gets away with his bluffs. Possibly Wall Street. A wise guy, a crisp guy, who can speak the words *recurrence*, *leukemia*, and *expiration* without losing confidence.

¤ ¤ ¤

THE TV REMOTE control gadget is clicking frantically on the other side of the curtain—a pathetic sound. I close my eyes and think of the chemical dripping into my blood, bathing me, coating my healthy cells, shielding them.

As once I thought I could shield my daughter from harm, even from torpor.

¤ ¤ ¤

I MUST HAVE nodded off. When I awake, afternoon shadows are lengthening. I hear slow, slippered steps, and my roommate shuffles around the curtain. I guess him to be in his mid- to late forties, his face pasty, his hair intact and, for the moment, still thick. His eyebrows are heavy and graying—Slavic? Greek?—and a broad field of hair sweeps down across his forehead, most of it black-gray. There's a handsome silver fringe down to where his hair is invaded by widow's peaks, or rather, hillocks. He's lean, on his way to gaunt. Hollow-cheeked. Six feet or taller but a trifle stooped—surprising for someone his age. He doesn't look like a plodder—more of a strider. He takes a step toward my bed, as if to shake my hand, and then pulls back.

"I'm supposed to keep my distance," he says, his voice so firm he could sandpaper cold steel into warm dust. He has a way of projecting that now makes me wonder if he's in the theater. He gives out a quick, crooked smile, producing a web of creases that fans out from the corners of his eyes, then retracts it.

"If you say so. How long have you been here?"

"I'm in day four of this round. My cells are slow to give up their secrets. I'm waiting for a definite diagnosis."

"Uh-huh." What does one say?

"Nothing to say, is there," he says, flashing another grin, then adds: "Welcome to the palace of cures," and scuffs his thinly slippered feet along the floor and into the bathroom.

¤ ¤ ¤

THE LIGHT OUTSIDE is reddening, the light inside is fluorescent, colorless, cold. I adjust my recline angle; the bed rumbles and ripples. I feel weak but content. The glow on the undistinguished brick and glass-steel combinations outside momentarily eclipses the chaos. Fellow citizens, frenetic, disgruntled, thinking that you deserve to be happy, or to pretend to be happy, pregnant, perhaps, or wanting to be pregnant, or not being pregnant, or agonized about being pregnant, or not exactly healthy but not sick either, you've done your best and worst, and there's nothing to do but replay the events of the day. It's the hour when most of the frantic world stops trying and now the backwash starts—your remorse at losing your temper, your fear that you are wasting your time, your sadness at not having done your best, your melancholy at being reminded of your failings. I'm alive to watch the shadows lengthen one more time.

I'm appreciating—nestling into—simplicity. I'm in a warm bed with clean sheets, and the world is stripped down to its—what? Do I believe there's a core? Still? The fairy-tale heart or the soul? Nietzsche seems to say there is no core—it's perspectives all the way down. In which case, why not relax and wait for the next perspective to offer itself? Hooked up to an IV line, I'm away from e-mail, voice mail, meetings, university clamor, bills, and visitors, each of whom, taken one at a time, might be welcome but in sequence make too many herky-jerky demands on my attention. I'm liberated from shelves full of unread books, an inbox overflowing with God knows what, desks groaning with unfinished business, the automatically expiring answers to the question of how to spend the next hour or the next evening, the question of how to proceed with Nietzsche. Face it: The country of health is crowded with obstacles, distractions, and vague clouds of ambition. Here, my body fills up with virulent chemicals, I offer up vital signs to nurses and greet occasional doctors, I eat, and I sleep. There's a clear-cut ambition for you: *sleep*.

But hold on: Too much simplicity is self-starvation. I'm controlled by subtraction, surrender. Slumped here through no fault of my own, I should make better use of these intervals of silence, as Nietzsche did. I should settle down in the moment and scribble a thought before it melts away—just for the sake of a smattering of definite here-and-now joy. There's always a thunderbolt to hurl at the page. Give him a trauma, he'll show you a style.

Sickness keeps him active, mobile. *Mein lieber* Fritz, the sick man of central Europe, roams here and there in fervent, futile search of relief, and when his headaches are incapacitating enough, his vomiting attacks so severe as to bring up blood, he drags himself to a clinic or a spa—always a different one. He contemplates even more strenuous regimens. He samples the miracle drugs of his time. He writes himself all manner of prescriptions as "Dr. Nietzsche." The drugs sometimes help. At Wagner's recommendation, he takes icy baths daily. He spends four weeks in a Black Forest clinic where he tries daily cold-water enemas, and eats four little meals consisting solely of meat, and drinks one glass of Bordeaux. He sits still while leeches are applied to his ears. None of these remedies do any good. A Swiss innkeeper recalls that his eccentric customer sometimes eats, in addition to one beefsteak, up to three kilos of fruit per day—"stone-hard plums and grass-green apples," he tells a reporter, years later, after Nietzsche has gone mad. "Naturally, no stomach can stand that!" the innkeeper adds. "Then he was sick and did not come for days. I often said to him, 'Professor, the fruit is what is making you sick.' 'No,' he then said, 'the meat; I can't stand your beefsteak'; and he laughed."

He tries "fletcherizing" his solid food—chewing it down to a liquid pulp, a fad popularized by Nietzsche's American contemporary Horace Fletcher, who liked to say: "Nature will castigate those who don't masticate"—it would have been surprising if Fritz hadn't given fletcherizing a shot. Henry James, Mark Twain, and Franz Kafka would all try it.

Nietzsche is no fool. He must be fully aware that the odds of improvement from the popular treatments of the late nineteenth century are decidedly less than even. Instead of wasting his time, he will make the most of his laughable life. He doesn't whine. Whether he finds himself in a Swiss mountain village or in the ochre repose of Turin, a moment will come when the flame licks up in his mind and he unscrews the cap of his fountain pen, or pecks away at his spanking-new state-of-the-art typewriting machine, and . . . writes. His mind is on fire. He burns through the entire philosophical history of his civilization. He piles up centuries, hell, millennia of errors and consigns them lovingly to the flames.

In search of a few days of lucidity—even a few hours—there's no border he won't cross. The atrophied life of the homebound whose ailments become their all-consuming professions is not for him. He is all too human enough to contemplate putting an end to himself once or twice, but such moments pass. The refugee keeps on the move, meets people on trains, impresses hikers with his quiet laughter, his courtesy, the twinkle in his unfocused eyes. He dashes from one inn to another, from train station to train station, crossing borders, crossing fingers, a homeless bomb-thrower, lighting one fuse after another under the smug nationalists and progress freaks, the fey nostalgics and lackluster academics, all of them so provincial as to imagine that they are destined to feel at home in the universe!

Never mind that he is stripped down to his quivering nerve endings. As he tramps around Europe, homeless, looking for a bearable climate, he devises a style to suit his peculiar condition. He writes in fifteen-minute bursts, in fits and starts, because he never knows when another detonation of pain is going to smash into the soft tissue behind his eyes, exploding his composure and with it his ability to pursue a protracted argument, and also because, in the midst of his sleepless nights, he has taken to scribbling notes to himself and piling them up by his bedside. The aphoristic style is perfect for him, for his great insight is that the world is an assemblage and not a unity. He chastises everyone from Plato to Wagner for hastening after the absolute. Not for this near-invalid the careless lope across fields of continuous dialectic—the "one long argument" practiced by his hero-nemesis Darwin, for instance, or lumbering Kant; or the self-indulgent logorrhea of Hegel. No, Nietzsche in his tossings and turnings and intervals between seizures—some of these seizures last for days—develops a new style: *literatus interruptus.*

Necessity swells his genius. He will be the maestro of discontinuous paragraphs. No mind has ever thought at such velocity, with such lightning shifts of direction. Mind thinks its way out of mind. The hell with transitions! Only the herd need footbridges. Nietzsche knows mountains. With every one of his breathless, breathtaking paragraphs, he leaps. He bounds over abysses. Reader, keep up if you can! He blurts out a staccato thought and leaves it dangling, humming with intimations and unfinished signals, gleeful with what does not have to be said *because he is Nietzsche.* Damned if he is going to slow down for the obvious and pick his way like a donkey down a thorny path of *if*s, *then*s, and *because*s!

And during respites, when the pain subsides or vanishes, and he rejoices, he will put to use the lessons he drew from his times of fitfulness. In fact, it's during a rare period of continuous happiness in 1882 that he composes his great aphoristic tribute to the "comedy of existence," *Joyful Knowledge.* During Genoa's mild winter, in an uninterrupted fervor, he learns how to climb from tragedy into comedy. Disruptions will be pitons, distractions will be ropes. He hoists his way to the next peak, and the next—

He writes to Lou Salomé: "Mind? What is 'mind' to me? What does knowledge matter? I treasure nothing except *impulses.*" Thinking is an improvisation that takes place beneath consciousness. It is not one of those plodding five-finger exercises with which most human beings content themselves. His messages will be deciphered, decipherable, only to readers who are willing to follow him without his having to fill in the blanks. So he will interrupt himself when he likes, start afresh, stagger forward, sideways, diagonally, leaving it to his secret sharers to lurch along behind him. If they can't keep up, they're the wrong readers. So suffering makes him an intuitionist and a tease.

And when it's time again to jump up from his desk, he does so without complaining. He heaves his guts out gladly. He catches his breath, drinks a glass of water, waits to see if he needs to purge himself again. Eventually he drags himself back to bed with cold compresses over his forehead. There he savors his superiority to the run of humanity. But he does not whine. He will not be one of those weaklings who pretend that their weakness is their personal strength. He will not be . . . no, he will *not* be . . . his father, who dropped dead at thirty-six. Like Prometheus, like Sisyphus, like—yes!—his nemesis Jesus, Fritz discovers that his strength lies in self-overcoming.

Further books will gush and swirl out of his pen. *The Genealogy of Morals*, for all its coherence, fails to purge or cure him. His leftover scribbles, collected as *The Will to Power*, are a fever chart. Of course, his books don't make Nietzsche well. Famously, he goes babbling mad in his forty-fifth year. But perhaps this denouement is his form of health. Without a doubt—isn't it obvious?—he does in his own life what he says all noble spirits need to do: He transvalues sickness. He overcomes his pathetic body without ever thriving—or rather, he invents a world in which his leaping and bounding spirit is redefined as the very spirit of health. I imagine him dancing out of his sickbed, flinging his arms in the air, whirling around—until, *smack*, he finds himself sprawled on the floor. Even then, he rejects bitterness. He finds his condition *hilarious*, like a fart or a loud sneeze. Self-pity would be sickness. He exults at his audacity. He permits himself what he calls "self-compassion." He becomes his own treatment. He is victorious. But he never forgets the difference between recovering from sickness and avoiding it in the first place. "Equally poised against death *and* life," he writes his dear Lou, "I brewed my medicine, concocted of my thoughts with their small stripe of unclouded sky above."

"Sickness itself can be a stimulant to life," he writes not long before losing his marbles, "only one must be healthy enough for this stimulant." He invites his readers to self-medicate. Nietzsche accomplishes this pedagogical feat with his ferocious will. It's as if no one since Jesus had ever mustered such excruciating resolve. In this way, he will make sure that his misery does not refute his philosophy. No one will be able to twit him with, "If you're so smart, how come you're not healthy?"

He is not trying to teach us how to live like him. But is he telling us, through his life work, what it would be like to be him? Or what it would be like to be a cured version of him? Or what it would be like to be ourselves?

⌑ ⌑ ⌑

IT'S GOING TO take shape, all right, this study of the roots of Nietzsche's thought in his ailments. *Nietzsche: The Health of a Sick Man.* Or perhaps, *The Ebullience of a Sick Man*, or *Archangel of the Sickbed.* A book the likes of which no one else has ever written:

Part I: Headaches
Part II: Eye Aches and Growing Blindness
Part III: Nausea and Vomiting

I don't know whether I'm kidding.

Archangel of the Sickbed, yes, this will be a worthy homage. Enough of these fussy, footnote-choked treatises wheezing under the burden of the tenure system! I'll make of each of my symptoms a springboard for insight, and thus delight, the accomplishment of my destiny. . . .

This is it, the blissful moment when the book-spark catches and pure excitement flares up into—

Each sentence I write now is an hors d'oeuvre inviting a hunger for more—

As for the main dish, I can wait. The starters are always the best part of the meal.

Speaking of which, I'm ravenous.

¤¤¤

I PUT DOWN my yellowing paperback of *Human, All Too Human*, a college keepsake and a relief from Kant, and study the menu. Which is less likely to be repulsive, crab cakes or Swiss steak?

The toilet flushes, and my roommate trudges back into the room, dragging his slippers across the floor. His nose is straight and sharp, his cheekbones sculpted, and he has the taut, sullen expression of a model or a drug addict. "If you like salt," he says in a voice flatter than before, "you'll love the crab cakes."

He flashes a smile as if by pressing a button. He is on his way back to his bed when he hesitates. His smile flickers and vanishes. "Mind if I sit down for a minute?" he says, and then after an interval: "I'm looking for a different perspective."

"Make yourself right at home," I say. He does, adjusting the visitor's chair so that he can swivel his eyes between the Queensboro Bridge and me. He looks back over his shoulder and out the window as if he's never noticed the bridge before.

"I'm Alan Meister."

"Garry McGinnis," he says, turning back to me. "Garry with two *r*'s." He searches me with moribund eyes, damp and gray as fog. "So who are you in civilian life?"

"Actually, I'm a philosopher."

"A philosopher." He rolls the word around in his mouth as if it were chocolate. "I took a couple of philosophy courses in college. They were too much for me. I'm not the type."

That makes me the type—does he mean logical? fussy? plodding? ascetic?—but I don't feel like arguing with him. Nor am I in a self-disclosing mood. I'm not in the hospital to bond with strangers. Not being much for small talk, I go silent, but it feels awkward, and he's clearly expecting more from me, so I decide to play Socrates in a minor key:

"What did you give it up for, then?"

"Poli sci. Then law. To spare me from the need to read books. I'm dyslexic. Now I'm paid to get other people to read for me."

These brazen guys who talk as though they're in charge of whatever it is they do, and deserve to be in charge because they know how to run the world—as a connoisseur of self-doubt I've always resented them, but at the same time I'm curious to know what it's like to feel that degree of entitlement. Garry McGinnis interests me. He struts, but at the same time there's a look in his eyes that I interpret as a deniable request for sympathy. So I say nothing.

"You get paid to think," he says.

I nod. "That's not to say that the university gets its money's worth, but yes, I get paid to think."

"Congratulations. Nice work."

"Thanks. I try."

"You try. . . . You remind me of Bogart's line to what's-his-name in *Casablanca*. 'We all try. You succeed.'" He speaks the line with a forced chuckle.

"You're too young to know *Casablanca* by heart."

He twists up the right side of his face, incredulous. This seems spontaneous, heartfelt. "I'm not as young as I look," he says. I see now how his face sags and his chin lacks definition. If this is as far as the conversation is going to go, I'd rather get back to Nietzsche.

"Personally," he goes on, "I avoid thinking whenever possible. I don't have time for it."

"Oh?"

"Too busy flying my desk."

Garry's laugh is younger than his face. There's something a bit desperate about his raucousness. There's a moment when his cheekbones tighten up and he looks as though he's on the verge of saying something else but thinks better of it.

"Well," he says after a pause, "see you around." He plods off, and a few seconds later from the other side of the curtain I hear the TV click on and the jabber of electronic noise.

⌑ ⌑ ⌑

After the lunch dishes are cleared and I've drunk enough water to wash the salt out of my mouth, Garry appears on my side of the curtain, saying, "Knock knock."

"Who's there?"

"Misery."

"Misery who?"

"Misery loves company."

That gets a laugh out of me. "Come on in," I say. He already has.

"Have a seat." He does, tilting the chair against the back wall next to the window. In the fluorescence, he looks on the greenish side of pale.

"So," he says briskly, "what brings you to this fabulous resort?"

"Lymphoma."

He tosses off a little salute. "Lymphoma, leukemia. How you doing?" He stares with a weird aggressiveness into my eyes, grins askew, then turns his head so he's gazing just to the side, as if my shadow were more interesting than my full face.

"I'm doing."

"Good for you. Me, I feel wasted, just like the first time, ten years ago. My doctor keeps saying he's not sure this time. I'm sure. I go with my gut."

"That's a long remission," I say idiotically.

"Suspended sentence."

I want to get back to *Human, All Too Human*, but something about Garry McGinnis tells me he needs conversation, so I'm willing to play along.

"You're a lawyer, I take it."

"Assistant DA. I put bad guys in jail."

No wonder he takes over a room.

"What's that like?"

"It's a great feeling. Rikers Island is full of animals who'll tell you how good we are. They don't get out on appeal. My losers stay losers. Last time I looked at the numbers, since I took over the unit we sent away forty-six murderers, one hundred nineteen rapists, four hundred something armed robbers, something like twenty-two hundred dealers, and yadda yadda."

"Impressive."

"You could fill Madison Square Garden with the families of all the individuals who didn't become victims because we put the bad guys in prison." He places the stress on *Square*, as I do—Madison *Square* Garden. He must come from the Bronx, like me.

"Must give you a great feeling," I say.

"Correct. And none of those individuals know my name, and you know what? That doesn't bother me in the slightest. Nothing can stop the guy who doesn't need credit for his accomplishments. I don't need a plaque."

This guy has a chip on his shoulder, and it isn't a microchip, it's actually more like a plaque.

"You're upbeat," I say lamely. "That's good."

"Winners stay winners. I know what I'm worth. They can't take that away from me. You know that song?"

"I remember it, yeah."

"That's my song. I like standards."

"Uh-huh."

"My boss used to say, like he was conveying the wisdom of the ages: 'Set your standards and stick to them, Garry. A lot of people won't get it. A lot of people *will* get it and say they approve—until the moment comes when it's their ox that's being gored, and then they'll scream, *Unfair!* Fuck 'em. They'll lift a glass to you when you're dead.' Standards—that's it. I want that engraved on my tombstone: *He Kept Standards*. Like, *He Kept a Tune*."

"I know what you mean."

"The losers can't take it, the politicians can't take it, the appeals court judges can't take that away from me. Sometimes the ACLU can't take it either. You're not a card-carrying member of the ACLU, are you?"

"I think I was once, but my membership lapsed. It was too boring."

⌑ ⌑ ⌑

A NURSE KNOCKS at the door. She's here to take vital signs. Garry hauls himself up and retreats behind his curtain, saying, "See you around."

"I'm not feeling so vital," I tell the nurse. She stares at me blankly. Must not speak English. What if I really needed help?

The sound of Court TV starts up again on the other side of the curtain, though blessedly muffled this time.

¤ ¤ ¤

I SCRIBBLE IN my notebook. I wonder what Nietzsche did when a loquacious fellow sufferer stepped into the spa waters alongside him. Did he hum Wagnerian arias? Explore the absurdity of the quest for truth? Chat about the respective techniques of the masseuses? Ask to be left alone? Did nineteenth-century Germans make small talk? Twentieth- and twenty-first-century Germans don't, in my experience. Contact with most people was hell for Nietzsche but he must have been polite. Maybe he chuckled for no apparent reason. Maybe they quieted down when they observed his vague, staring, cavernous eyes and decided he must be more than a bit *off*.

The woman on Garry's TV rattles on. I wad up strips of tissue and stuff the wads into my ears. I reflect that Garry McGinnis is a man with a lot on his mind, and I don't think it's only leukemia.

I imagine my minuscule grandchild floating in Natasha's amniotic fluid. Is it time for a beating heart and buds where limbs will be? I try to imagine her as a mother, loving, steady, attentive. I imagine her as she is, passionate and erratic. Like her father. I drift off.

¤¤¤

"SORRY, YOU BUSY?" says Garry. If the nurse's visit dampened him, you'd never know it, since he's got his take-charge voice back.

"Not really," I say, putting my notebook down. "This is how I while away the hours."

"Actually," he says as if I hadn't spoken, "this woman Nancy Grace annoys me no end. She's supposed to have been a prosecutor once upon a time. So how come she moves her mouth in that hysterical way?"

"You know, I've never watched her."

"It's such crap. How come she never talks about the hard choices that a real prosecutor makes?" he says. "All the cases you have to go up with absent the evidence you want, when your Plan B is a pathetic plea bargain that you know is a bad idea? What are you going to do about the jurors who simply can't believe that that nice-looking white individual wearing the finely knotted tie and trim double-breasted suit is a vicious scumbag of a rapist?"

I'm thinking that I've been appointed Garry McGinnis's father-confessor, and I don't know how to resign this position I never applied for.

"Instead of her over-the-top screeching, this woman might win some respect for prosecutors if she talked straight once in a while about political interference with the criminal justice system—the same criminal justice system that each and every one of her viewers relies on to keep the muggers, the rapists, and the drug dealers out of their neighborhoods. She could take some shots at reporters who can always find something more urgent to write about than what goes down in the courthouse. She could inform her audience about the horrible little cubicles that the staff has to work in. She could talk about how we can't recruit the most able law school graduates in the first place and then we lose our best assistant DAs to the white-shoe law firms. About how we can't find secretaries who know how to spell because the public schools don't have time to teach spelling, they're too busy giving out di*ver*sity training and—well, you know. How about the budget cuts and broken-down air-conditioning? How about the hack judges, all those political appointments that bubble up to the level of their incompetence and past it?"

He glances at me as if he's just remembered he has a witness, and says, "I don't mean to bore you. I know the answer, anyway. Nobody would watch."

"Believe me, I appreciate the distraction. So you sound like maybe you miss Giuliani."

"Yeah, maybe I do." He grins evasively like, in fact, Giuliani. "So you probably want to know, why am I spending my time watching Court TV, the freak show for people who like to say, 'Now I've seen everything'? The truth is, it bothers me a lot that I'm interested in this idiot woman. I feel like I'm rubbernecking at the scene of the accident. I must be sick. I am sick."

To this I have nothing to say.

"People keep telling me that it's only a bump in the road."

"I can see why they would say that."

"Good thing I've got my seat belt on." He snorts. "You sure I'm not going on too long."

"No, really, feel free."

"Bumps are my middle name," he resumes. "I lost my first high school debate. I lost my first murder prosecution. I lost my first armed robbery conviction on appeal. I lost out on a Yankee Stadium skybox when the department informed me that corporate donations of season tickets violate ethics rules. I lost my first wife. I lost my mother, for that matter, when I was twelve. I was sad, but to tell you the truth, I realized one day that she had lost me, so we were even. I never threw in the towel. My father was a fighter. Semipro, till he was knocked out one too many times. Just as well—he went to college, got his degree, then he got a master's, started teaching community college. He taught me you should always record your wins and your lessons and not your losses."

He's waving his hands now, which is hard to do when you've got an IV stuck in the back of your hand.

"So you notice I'm not saying a word about my stepmother. But moving on: I made the debate team, and we won the citywide medal. About baseball, I learned to throw screwballs. About track, I learned how to save myself for the last half mile and I won the Bronx half marathon. I learned what to ask on voir dire about the admissibility of circumstantial evidence, and I won twenty-six cases in a row that I prosecuted on circumstantial evidence. I made chief assistant DA at thirty-five. I beat acne before I was twenty, jock itch before I was thirty, and leukemia before I was forty."

"You take my breath away."

"Thank you. And I'm going to win this time. And I can tell you're gonna win, too." He skips a beat. "I can tell."

His phone rings. "Later," he says, and slogs to the other side of the curtain. His voice booms:

"Fine, fine, couldn't be better. Ha-ha. Don't worry, the cure will be better than the disease. . . . I don't know, you know what I think? I think, one day at a time. I think it's the bottom of the seventh and I'm behind but I've got the bases loaded and my cleanup guy's coming up. Watch out."

"I'll catch you later," he finally says.

⌑ ⌑ ⌑

ANOTHER NURSE BUSTLES in, a short, chubby one with a pile of blonde hair, to check my catheters, accompanied by a doctor I also haven't seen before, a skinny clean-shaven guy who scarcely looks old enough to read a thermometer. Every time I turn around there's somebody different poking me.

"You're about the fourth one today," I say to the nurse.

"Yes," replies the doc, "but she's the one the insurance pays for."

"Oh? Who pays for the others?"

No answer. They're too busy to make conversation. You don't want to get them started on the economics of medicine. They've got a floor full of afflicted people to tend to.

⌑ ⌑ ⌑

QUIET DESCENDS ON Garry McGinnis's side—no phone voice, no Court TV, but, as I pay attention, a slow, regular, quiet wheeze. I'm relieved to share my solitude with Nietzsche, who confesses that he *invented* once upon a time

> the "free spirits" to whom this discouragingly encouraging book with the title *Human, All Too Human* is dedicated. There are no such "free spirits" nor have there ever been any, but, as already said, I needed them for company to keep me cheerful in the midst of evils (sickness, loneliness, foreignness, acedia, inactivity) as brave companions and ghosts with whom I could laugh and gossip when I so desired and send to the devil when they became bores—as compensation for the lack of friends.

⌑ ⌑ ⌑

It's morning in Sloan-Kettering. Light seeps tentatively into the room. I slept well: Whatever they pumped into me last night worked. Another nurse arrives before breakfast, hangs a new bag of chemicals on my pole, and plugs it into the line that runs into the back of my hand. I investigate the haze of my mind, and find more haze, but as the room brightens, the haze becomes warmer, more comforting. I glance at the front page of the paper.

Before any news rubs off on me, I have to admit I feel a certain pleasure from waking up in the hospital. If I were Nietzsche, I'd go right to work—after all, the revaluation of all values depends on me. But I'm Alan Meister, two months into the chemotherapy phase of existence. Life is stripped down to me and the chatty stranger who drops in from time to time. I have no errands or appointments. The news of the world, my daughter's quandaries, the question of whether I'm doing right by my students, the question of whether I have anything much of interest to say about Nietzsche and illness—all that is a background blur. I think of my future grandchild's tiny toes and chubby little legs. I take my meals, I submit to probes, I answer questions, I ring for assistance, I sleep.

⌑ ⌑ ⌑

"Do ME A favor and open the curtain, would you?" I say as Garry drags back from the bathroom.

He does. The sun is coming up over the corrugated surface of the East River. The waters ripple with brightness. At this moment, Garry McGinnis and I, in our luxury suite, are among the privileged, perched high over the coast of Manhattan with a clear view of the bridge, the glimmering river, the tugboats, the industrial remnants on the other shore. Off to the south, an indifferent sea.

"You mind if I ask you a question?" he asks.

"You just did. And I don't mind."

There's something about Garry McGinnis that brings out the high school kid in me.

This draws a quick snort. "You ever think you made a bad decision, and then, every which way you replay it, you realize you had no alternative? You were just fucked from the start?"

I mumble noncommittally, but I want to keep him talking, so I toss in: "You know, yesterday you claimed I was a big success. But if you met my daughter, the college dropout, you might not think I was such a big success. So I imagine I made some bad decisions along the line, too, though damned if I know exactly what they were."

He's one of these guys who thinks in dialogue, talks in dialogue—a man who lives in relation to others. He sits down and turns to his captive audience.

"THAT NURSE LAST night, the four by four, she reminded me of a witness I took a chance on in a case. You know? When you don't have a gun in a gun murder case, you find an eyewitness. When you don't have an eyewitness, you go for the next best thing. When you don't have the next best thing, you go for broke. This witness—funny, I can't remember her name, but she looked like a truck—whatever her name was, she wasn't the next best thing, she was the only thing.

"This perp Carlos Ortiz was a real piece of work, a first-rate prospect for life without parole. I had a case I felt pretty good about. I can taste these things. I had not one but two first-degree murders, I had a motive, I had an opportunity, I had an unattractive defendant, I had a whole story. *People of the State of New York v. Ortiz* involved a pretty straightforward crime of passion. Correction: a *very* straightforward crime of passion. You sure you don't mind me going on like this?"

"Not at all. Go right ahead."

"Thanks. OK. So one of the victims is named Lucy. She's Carlos's girlfriend, she's on welfare, she lives with her son on Third Avenue way uptown. The other victim is Lucy's son, a punk in his twenties—a dealer, actually. A dealer in marijuana. They're all Puerto Ricans, not that it matters. Carlos lives in the South Bronx, but his wife threw him out of the house a few years before and he was living on the street in East Harlem when he ran into Lucy. Anyway, Carlos and Lucy liked each other, one thing led to another, and they got it on. Eventually Carlos goes back to his wife but he keeps up a thing with Lucy on the side. For a schlumpy kind of guy he must have a way about him, but what do I know about women? He's a retired jeweler, he owns the building he lives in, he takes care of his bedridden father, who's got his own basement apartment, but he has lots of time on his hands. So a few afternoons a week he drives down to visit Lucy in Spanish Harlem and then he stays over with her, then wakes up the next morning, or noon, whatever, and wanders down the street to play dominoes with the locals, then he heads home to the Bronx. So life goes on like that for Carlos—pretty cozy if you ask me."

"What about the wife?"

"The wife, right. Apparently Lucy and the wife came to some kind of arrangement, they even had a sit-down together once—the wife is some kind of iron lady—and life goes on like this for years until, one day, Carlos gets word that Lucy's been seen with another guy. No question, Carlos sees his sweet deal going sour. How would you feel? So, a week or two later, Carlos is visiting Lucy as usual and there's a huge fight in Lucy's apartment. The next-door neighbors hear yelling and screaming. Carlos pulls out a gun and shoots Lucy and her son to death in the kitchen. Eleven shots. One of the bullets goes through the kitchen wall and rips into the belly of a young girl who's partying next door, though she lived."

He's on a roll, is Garry McGinnis. He leans forward in his seat, and his voice booms as he charges deeper into his saga, and he's gazing off slightly away from me again, in a bit of a trance, as if my reaction doesn't matter, which it pretty clearly doesn't, but I don't mind because I'm enthralled.

"This is where my star witness comes in—Miss Four by Four, whatever. She lives one floor down, and she testifies that she's standing outside her door, on the landing, while her grandkids are playing on the roof, and she hears what sounds to her like a gunshot, and then more gunshots, eleven, twelve shots, she loses count, and she suddenly realizes that she's lost track of the kids, she doesn't know where they've gone, so she runs up the stairs on her way to the roof, and when she passes the stairwell exit to the next floor the door is open and she sees something out of the corner of her eye, so she stops to look and she sees Carlos Ortiz, who she immediately recognizes as a regular visitor to the building—they're on a friendly basis—she sees Carlos charge out of Lucy's apartment and tear-ass down the hall to the staircase on the far side. She's sure that it's Carlos. We go through this a hundred times. So I've got a motive, which is great, and I've got his prints all over the apartment, fine, and the only alibi he's got is his wife, who says he was with her the whole time, but she's his wife, after all. What isn't so great is that I don't have an eyewitness to the shooting and I don't have a weapon, but I have two eyewitnesses to Carlos on his way out of the apartment where his girlfriend is lying in a pool of blood."

"Two witnesses," I chime in. I'm riveted.

"Right. I'll get to my other beaut in a minute. So now we come to trial, in that usual speedy way we know and love so well, something like a year Carlos Ortiz is in the slammer, but never mind—So anyway, I put Señorita Four by Four on the stand, and her story starts falling apart. Yes, she was watching her grandchildren, but while she was watching them—or pretending to watch them—it turns out that she was hanging out with her boyfriend on the landing. She never said anything about a boyfriend before. OK.

"Suddenly there's a boyfriend, and while they're out there on the landing they're drinking beer. Or actually she's drinking beer while he's drinking bourbon.

"'Oh,' says the defense, like he's just struck gold, which he has, 'and how much beer would you say you drank in the course of the afternoon?' He's taking a stab in the dark. He never laid eyes on this chiquita before. He's never heard a word about beer. It wasn't like I ever heard it before, either. So anyway, 'I don't know,' she says. 'Well, was the beer cold?' 'Oh, sure. I wouldn't drink warm beer!' Like she's offended. She's trying to be helpful, and what kind of a screwball does he think she is? 'But you don't remember how much you drank in the course of the afternoon.' 'No, sir.' 'Well, Miss Whatsis'—Ramirez, that's it—'well, Miss Ramirez, do you recall taking the beer out of the refrigerator?' 'Oh sure.' 'And how much beer was it that you removed from the refrigerator?' 'I think it was six.' 'Six bottles?' 'No, it was cans.'

'You took six cans of beer out of the refrigerator, then?' 'No, six-packs.'

"Six six-packs. This loser of a court-appointed attorney can't believe his luck. 'You took six six-packs out of the refrigerator and you carried it out to the hallway.' 'Uh-huh.' 'And your boyfriend didn't drink any of that beer.' 'No, he don't like beer. He likes bourbon.' With a smile. 'And so you drank the beer,' the defense attorney says. She shrugs. 'It was a hot day.' 'I see your point,' he says. 'And how many cans of beer would you say you drank that afternoon, Miss Ramirez?' 'Don't know exactly.' 'What would you estimate?' I object. The judge sustains me. But I'm not going to get away with it.

"No, I wouldn't think so," I slip in edgewise.

"So he asks her, 'Did you drink up all the beer in those six six-packs?' 'Oh no, your honor.' Like, what kind of lady does he think she is? He gets cute. 'I'm not your honor,' he says, 'I'm just the defense attorney. Miss Ramirez, what did you do with the beer you didn't drink?' 'Put it back.' 'Back where?' 'In the refrigerator.' 'I see. And how many cans did you put back in the refrigerator?' 'Ten.'

"This is embarrassing. I'm sitting there helpless while the guy shreds my witness. This is one for the books. 'You returned ten cans of beer to the refrigerator?' 'Uh-huh.' 'And you started with six six-packs.' 'I told you.' 'So you started with thirty-six cans of beer, and when you were done, there were ten cans of beer left.' 'That's right.' 'So you drank twenty-six cans of beer that afternoon?' 'I guess so.'

"'And how many hours were you standing out there on the landing with your boyfriend drinking?' 'I don't know. A few hours.' 'A few hours.' 'Three, four hours, something like that.' 'Something like that.'"

Garry McGinnis gazes straight at me. "You're thinking this is better than *Law & Order*, right? A genuine meltdown moment."

"I don't know, I never watch it, I'm more the *Perry Mason* vintage."

"OK. It gets worse. Lawyer goes on shooting fish in a barrel, pop, pop, pop. He's checked Ramirez out and he knows she has mental problems and in fact, she's just a couple of months out of the loony bin. He pushes her on why she was in the loony bin, and it turns out that she was hearing voices. All kinds of voices. Oh no, she wasn't hearing voices the day Lucy and her son were shot to death. Not then. 'Thank you very much, Miss Ramirez. No further questions.' And I'm the guy who stocked the fish in that particular barrel.

"And then it gets worse. Now I have to tell you about my other key witness, the security guard. Ah, the security guard. On the day of the killings this young gentleman is sitting at a card table in the lobby keeping track of comings and goings. He testifies that he sees Carlos Ortiz come roaring down out of the stairwell, all out of breath and frantic. Carlos screeches to a stop when he sees through the window that a police car is parked in front and the cops are getting out of the car and heading into the building, so he runs out the other door into the courtyard. He doesn't come back. There's a fence on the other side of the courtyard which he could climb, and then he could make his way to his car and drive back to the Bronx.

"Only thing is, the defense attorney, who's no genius, I know these guys—anyway, he figures out from the jumpsuit my security guard is wearing on the stand that he's no longer a security guard, that he is in fact in the custody of the city of New York awaiting trial for heroin sales, and I've written a to-whom-it-may-concern letter commending his service to the People, a copy of which is duly submitted into evidence."

Underneath his unbroken, outspoken boldness, Garry is showing signs of embarrassment. The bags under his eyes have darkened.

"And then it gets worse," he goes on. "It didn't look so good for my case that Carlos has had three heart attacks, and he's overweight—even after eleven months in jail awaiting trial he's still on the chunky side—while we're in the position of having to convince the jury that he climbed over an eight-foot fence to get out of the courtyard. And him without a mark on his body, according to the police, who examined him after they picked him up, except for the marks that, let's face it, they probably put there in the effort to get a confession out of him. Which I'm not saying I condone."

"So when you realized the case was so thin, why not look elsewhere?"

"A very good question for the police, which I'm not. A lot of people might have had motives. Lucy's kid was a dealer, and he had a reputation for selling bad dope—did I mention that? He might have burned somebody. He might have burned more than one somebody. Somebody might have wanted to get even, and Lucy might have got caught in the middle. The bullets that killed them, most of them hit vital organs, like it was a professional job, not a crime of passion. I knew all this. But I don't have a police department at my disposal. What else could I have done with this fucking case? I had two corpses and one suspect—what was I supposed to do, walk away? Dismiss the case in the interests of justice?"

I accepted his unstated invitation to chime in, or at least to play straight man. "Well, you didn't have a confession. You had a guy who pled not guilty."

"Most assholes plead not guilty. It's the American way. I had Carlos's prints all over the apartment. But if you ask what that was worth, I'd have to agree that he didn't deny having been a regular over there. I didn't have any gun. A jeweler usually owns a gun but he wasn't working anymore, and I didn't have any evidence that he owned a gun now. Let's face it, the cops picked up Carlos because he was a gimme: the suspect who fell into their hands, the jealous boyfriend, with only his wife as his alibi (although you had to admit it was a hell of a thing that she would testify for her husband when she knew he was shacking up with Lucy, but you know, it takes all kinds), and once he was locked up they could close the case and win brownie points, and that was that. What was I going to do? You prosecute the case you have, not the case you'd like to have. If I was running the NYPD—as my dad used to say. Don't get me started."

"So what happened?"

"The jury took an hour and a half to acquit. Well, like they say in the judicial instructions, reasonable doubt is doubt for which you can give a reason. They had their reasons. Do I think Carlos Ortiz is innocent? I didn't have the stuff to prove he was guilty. My witnesses were for shit. Carlos is a sad sack, kind of simpático, he takes care of his elderly father and all that. Live and learn. So what are we left with? This individual spends eleven months in jail awaiting trial because he can't make bail—eleven months during which his kid comes down with hepatitis and his wife has a nervous breakdown—and then, after two weeks at trial, the fucking jury takes an hour and a half to acquit, and I feel like an asshole, and the whole courtroom thinks I'm an asshole, and I can tell by the smug looks on the jury that they think I'm an asshole, too. Well, that's their privilege—it's a free country. I had a feeling about that jury in the first place: the pregnant nurse, the college professor, the Puerto Rican—but I'm not going to go there. So what was I supposed to do? So if I bring the guy to trial and then the jury cuts my balls off, so it cuts my balls off. That's your tax dollars at work, so I do my best and eat my heart out."

"It's rough," is all I can say. "To have that kind of responsibility." I think to myself: *Responsibility. I wonder if that word ever crossed Nietzsche's lips without contempt.*

"Tell me about it. And just by the way, if Carlos Ortiz didn't kill Lucy and her kid after all—just for the sake of argument—then who did? Because somebody did. And if Carlos Ortiz didn't do it, and you didn't do it, and I didn't do it, then whoever did do it is still out there on the street. While the cops are putting out press releases to prove that the city's getting safer by the minute, does anybody haul their butt out of a chair to give a shit? And I'm supposed to feel bad about trying the guy, now, because I have leukemia again. Give me a fucking break. You know, I'm tired of Carlos Ortiz and I don't feel like thinking about him for one more second."

Garry McGinnis stares at me, or off to the side of me, and there's a brief, dull sadness in his eyes, but then he flashes me an oblique grin, as if to say he's said too much, or not enough, or there are more problems lurking in the shadows of this story than he's even aware of, or maybe he's wondering why he brought up the subject of Carlos Ortiz in the first place. This wasn't a confession, exactly, but what was it? A dry run for an inconclusive deathbed speech? Is this what has become of confession among the irreligious, a kind of zero-commitment ramble in which you clear your moral decks with a stranger without committing yourself or even owning up that that's what you're doing? Cancer hospitals as the barrooms of our time?

I don't ask. He doesn't tell.

¤ ¤ ¤

Awkward moments ensue until breakfast arrives, full of watery orange juice and other false promises, and Garry takes the chance to retreat to the other side of the curtain without committing himself.

"Thank you for taking me into your confidence," I say as he lumbers away, because I have to say something.

"You're a good audience," is his exit line.

A good audience. Is this the reason why people are always telling me stories—they can sense I'm a sucker for them? My daughter, my colleagues, my partner in cancer—I'm omnivorous, or prurient. It's obvious to me once I think about it. Perhaps the truth is that my own inner life is impoverished, wizened, so I am required to feed on the experience of others. But Melanie doesn't think I'm such a good listener. She accuses me of interrupting—*Brutus interruptus*, she calls me. She's right, I do interrupt her. But it's not because I'm a brute. She doesn't understand that barging in is how, in a Jewish family, you show you're paying attention. You make it known that you're still there, all ears. Even a story requires punctuation. In any case, I do listen to stories. I revel in the entanglements. I despise the expression *Cut to the chase.* I don't want to cut: I want to paste.

But I don't know how to feel, exactly, about Garry's soliloquy. I'm impressed when somebody makes an effort at honesty, especially somebody who is good at dissembling. I know how hard it is to know what you deeply feel. On the other hand, maybe instead of letting him vent I should have challenged him. He does seem to be an Old Faithful of verbal eruptions. Still, he didn't just vent; he flowed. Filling the air to avoid the subject of leukemia, I suppose, and who can blame him?

But when he started this soliloquy, he said something about making a bad decision, then thinking it through and realizing that there was no alternative. It's peculiar, then, that I didn't hear about any bad decision in the Ortiz story. The way he told it, this was a story of a case that was bad from the start and not a story of a hard decision he had to make. What was he leaving out? There's no decision to make at this late date. Garry McGinnis doesn't strike me as a guy who revisits his moves. He's an action figure—kick ass and don't look back.

So maybe the Ortiz story was a smoke screen, evasive action. Maybe Garry is really brooding about something else. Maybe what he maybe sorta wanted to talk about and ended up not talking about was something absolutely different. Garry is not a guy who comes clean very often. He's a compartmentalizer. Talking is his way of not talking. Half the time he doesn't know why he's talking—

It's while I'm scarfing down my oatmeal that this notion hits me: Think of those two calls he got. He doesn't strike me as a tender-hearted guy, but both times his manner was, well, tender. The tone he took with them, he didn't take with the third caller, or with me. Both women, in other words. With the first one, he's a little remote, but he asks solicitously about "the little one." The other woman has a name, June, and to her he says he's not coming home today. He has a home with June. He has a child with someone who isn't June. He's on intimate terms with both of them.

I've read about these guys. They exist. The Stanford professor of medicine whose two wives, one from Northern California, one from Southern California, show up at the funeral. The prominent San Francisco lawyer whose estate ends up in splendid litigation between *his* two. Louis Kahn, the architect, with his *three* women, each bringing up one of his children, none of whom knows about the others. There are even bigamist women. Before these immensities my imagination breaks down.

I'm a melodramatist. One reason I get along with Nietzsche. But Nietzsche does it all with ideas. Ideas babble to him.

⌑⌑⌑

PEOPLE WILL NEVER fail to surprise you even in the ways they tease your imagination.

I page my way through the paper over soggy toast and acceptable coffee, and my mind drifts back to Carlos Ortiz and—of all things—my moral good luck. Truth is, I don't have, or want, multiple wives. I've never kept an innocent man in jail for even one month, and I can't imagine giving a speech like Garry's. Does this make me Nietzsche's complacent bourgeois after all?

But wait a minute. I've lived, I've lied, I've fucked around. If I were in a mood to confess, I could do some confessing. My sprees of bad temper directed at Melanie. The typical botch job of parenting. My all-around ingratitude, certainly—ingratitude for life. But the truth is, I feel inadequate anguish. If I'm twisted inside, it's in a simple, elegant way, Möbius-style. I don't have Carlos Ortiz's problems, not even close. Or even Garry's, I think.

⌑ ⌑ ⌑

MOST OF THE day: quiet. Melanie stops in after breakfast, holds my hand, tells me about calls from concerned friends and relatives. I'm alert enough to be reading Kant, dutifully, when she walks in, and the first thing she says is, "I should have brought the camera!" Natasha feels better and is going to visit later. No, she's not saying anything about the father of her child, and no, Melanie doesn't want to push her. Danny called from Tel Aviv, said he will be in New York in two weeks, at the time of my second ICE treatment; he'll visit me. Melanie is full of that mixture of blitheness and sobriety that I loved in her from the start. I introduce her to Garry on his way to the bathroom. He looks her up and down appreciatively.

I doze on and off. Garry doesn't reappear. Maybe on subsequent passages to the bathroom he sees that I'm sleeping and adjusts his habits accordingly. I'm disappointed, actually. I'm curious about the wives. I want the confession to go into extra innings.

Then I'm awakened from a late afternoon doze by a knock at the door so hesitant that I'm not sure it's a knock at all; then after a pause, there are several more knocks, each a bit louder than the last, and a surgically masked face pokes around the corner.

"Hello?"

It's not hard to recognize my one and only child, even masked. Her bony skinhead skull sprouts a coat of dark fuzz. She wears a jean jacket, slender jeans, and a long-hanging key chain. It's a guy's outfit, I think.

"Mom got tied up, so I'm the understudy." She speaks haltingly, as if this is a special occasion, a ceremonial pilgrimage, though neither of us knows exactly the rites of the occasion. Or maybe she's afraid that I'm going to bawl her out. The way she stands, with her pelvis strangely protruding, she looks as though she were dancing the feeling *I don't belong here*. But then I can't remember the last time she looked as though she belonged anywhere.

"I'm glad to see you. Come on over here. I'm not contagious."

She approaches the bed, bends over, and we arrange a thwarted hug.

"I really appreciate the solidarity," I say.

"What?"

I run my hand over my skull.

"Oh. Sure. Here, I brought you an iPod." Her manner is brisk. She must be suppressing the fright and dread that I would be feeling in her place. I'm touched, even if, for all I know, it's her mother who prodded her to visit and wire me for sound.

"Thank you. I'll try it."

She gazes at the two sacks of chemicals hanging from the pole, follows the IV tubes into the back of my hand. She goes silent, possibly awestruck. Perhaps she expects a fatherly homily about living a worthy life. Perhaps she expects me to disparage her gift on the ground that serious people don't require a soundtrack—if they need one, they have it running around their heads all the time, like Nietzsche with Wagner.

"I realize this is a sacrifice," I say.

"Oh—no, not really. It's a new one. I still have mine." Both of us are embarrassed.

How are you getting along, etc. etc. *I'm getting along fine, piece of cake*, etc. etc.

"So," she says crisply, dropping down into the visitor's chair. "What's happening?"

"Pull up the chair and talk to me."

She moves the chair closer to the bed, and we both wait.

"Talk to me," I interject into the silence.

"You mean, open up my mouth and make meaningful sounds?"

"That would work."

"OK, about being preggers, I feel fine. About your—cancer thing, I'm relieved."

I am wondering if Garry McGinnis has put not only me but my half of the room in a mood for revelations of the heart.

"And about your, uh, next—steps?"

"Easy, please."

"You know, you can stay with us as long as you want. That's not a question."

"Thank you. Mom already said so, but I appreciate it."

"Right. And. When are we going to meet him?"

"Pardon?"

"You know. The father."

"I wish you wouldn't."

"You mean, ask or meet him?"

"I guess both."

"Is he in the picture?"

"Can we pause it here?"

"What's the matter, Natasha?"

"Please don't push me."

"He has tattoos all over? He's a drug addict?"

"Nothing like that."

"A fundamentalist Christian?"

"Dad, I really don't want to talk about him. Yet. Can we talk about something else?"

Evidently not. The city beyond the hospital window turns velvet black, and the lights along the bridge have never looked brighter, like diamonds on the neck of a beautiful woman. Oh, darkness is good for the Queensboro Bridge, its outline etched in unyielding light, glamorous with the whorish promise of the electrified city, tarted up with so much impersonal charm, enclosing so much alluring and frantic life that it can withstand interruptions from the sick, the dying, and the dead.

Irresistible sleepiness overtakes me. I wish my daughter good night and sink into oblivion thinking how pleasant it is to have no alternative but sleep.

¤ ¤ ¤

January 26

Morning. The sacks of toxin are emptying out. I wonder how to ask Garry to clarify the matter of his wives. I don't want to express either aggression or wicked prurience; I just want a take-home gift. I expect it. After his Carlos Ortiz story, surely we're bosom buddies. But what if he doesn't come right out with it? What if he decides that he was too intimate with his professional problems yesterday and realizes that I might have overheard his phone conversations, and puts two and two together, and ducks behind a veil of reticence? He could work up a story to explain away what I heard with my own ears. In my imagination I try out various sidling-up techniques, unobtrusive cross-examinations. For naught—Garry doesn't put in an appearance.

A nurse arrives to tell me I'm repaired enough to have earned the right to go home. Then she pulls aside the curtain. Garry's bed is empty. She starts tidying up. His glasses, a candy bar, a pack of gum, and (I see now) a jigsaw puzzle are still on his little table overhanging the bed. So he hasn't—expired. I ask her where Mr. McGinnis is. "He's getting tested this morning," she says. Scanned. Which means that the odds are that I'll never see him again to find out how many wives he has.

Melanie comes for me, bringing her brisk good cheer. On the way out of the hospital, I pick up my homecoming present—an elixir called Neulasta, which I'm to inject into my belly. My belly.

In the cab, going home, I tell Melanie my theory about Garry's wives. She says I'm projecting my own desire. "I don't know why you guys bother," she says. "In the dark we're all the same."

"Ha-ha," I say.

Neulasta is a biotech concoction that prevents a particular kind of infection to which chemo patients are prone. Pick up a prefilled syringe, measure off three inches from your navel, swab the skin with alcohol, squeeze the syringe, empty it, then, when you're done, press the plunger again so that the syringe seals itself (the genius of our design culture!), stow the used syringe in a milk carton, and think of the whole process as another task of the day, like brushing your teeth.

⌑ ⌑ ⌑

January 29

Saturday night is basketball night. Although the Knicks have lost twelve out of their last fourteen games, anticipation is sweet.

They lose to Detroit, 91–61. That which did not destroy them did not make them stronger. Half the team is out with injuries. Frailty afflicts all us professionals. Natasha, who humors me by sharing the couch for the game, says I have a penchant for lost causes. *You're right: Look how I've stuck with you,* I resist saying.

If I didn't see another spring, I would regret it—who knows, the Knicks might come to life—but then, once I was gone, I would not be there to regret anything. Talking to Melanie, I insist that I'm not afraid of dying. But am I suppressing a sense that I've already lived long enough?

⌑ ⌑ ⌑

Monday, February 7

Back to Sloan-Kettering for ICE, round two. This time I bring along Rousseau's *Second Discourse on Inequality* and *The Social Contract*. Thursday I have to talk to my class about Rousseau's relation to the French Revolution. I'm in a different room than last time, and the TV on the other side of the curtain is silent.

Danny arrives after lunch, all moral intensity and warm-hearted exuberance, from Tel Aviv. He takes every chance to escape the Israeli pressure cooker and is here for an unremarkable political theory conference. Beneath his mask, he's beaming. Stocky and muscular, he always carries himself as if he knows his way around—he could pass for a surgeon. He looks up and down the plastic line conducting the fluid into the back of my hand and says, "Good, soon you'll be back on the battlefield." He sees *The Social Contract* lying on the little table next to the bed and frowns beneath his mask. He approves of Rousseau as a writer but not as a thinker:

"You know, Burke called Rousseau an 'insane Socrates,' 'deranged,' and he also said *The Social Contract* was 'a performance of little or no merit,' and though Burke had many fantasies, he was right this time." He is waving his outstretched index fingers around, conducting an invisible orchestra.

"It's wonderful to see you, Danny."

"Look, the magic way that the so-called, eh, general will appears and the individuals dissolve into it is, is, is, eh, like the religious burning—what do you call it?—self-immolation that we hate. Suicide bombing, even."

Which gives me an opening to tell him about my Nietzsche project. As I expected, he disapproves. As long as we've known each other, he's disapproved of my taste in philosophy. If you wonder what we have in common, it's our shared distaste for God. Danny grants Nietzsche that much. But overall he sees Nietzsche as a narcissist who spent his life hunting for a theoretical crutch to help him limp out of a personal abyss. Nietzsche is not the new beginning he claimed to be but a dead end in the history of Western individualism. Danny's residual Marxism is speaking, a prejudice for which I have a soft spot, but I can recognize sentimentalism when I see it.

"Let me put it this way," I say. "What is there to be said for the nineteenth century? Slavery, colonialism, gross poverty, epidemics, and wars that killed hundreds of thousands of people. The main thing is, it staved off the twentieth, which slaughtered tens of millions."

"Yah? So?"

"So this. Here's Nietzsche, the most intelligent man of the age. There's idiocy on every side. There's idiocy masquerading as passion and idiocy masquerading as big, grunting morality. All the herds are fattening on their own stupidity and sluggishness—the religious herds, the nationalist herds, the little herds of small-minded philosophers, the herds of millenarian socialists. He listens to them lowing and grunting, each at its own frequency."

"I hope you're enjoying this."

"I am, as a matter of fact. Now I'm going to switch metaphors on you. The atmosphere is noxious, and he's the canary in the mine. He's a canary with a great mind. He gets a whiff and he says, 'The hell with them all, I'm taking the trap door.' It wasn't his fault that nobody else followed, or hardly anyone else. What did he care? Sooner or later, if there were any successors worth a damn, they'd know that they need him. They'd read him because he'd be their only hope—"

"Tell me, what kind of hope? You know, I really don't see it. I see in Nietzsche no hope at all for humanity. I see an emergency exit for a few fortunate souls, period. A trap door into the void."

"You prefer the fantasy wonderland of the Marxists? The happy-ending history club?"

"To the exclusive club of escape artists, I do."

"You're kidding yourself, Danny. Nobody lives in that wonderland. Nobody ever did. You're no different from me, except that you won't acknowledge that you need to parachute out, too."

"Speak for yourself."

"You know I'm speaking for you, too. Trust me."

"And look how well the Germans did with his line of argument."

"That's cheap and you know it. You know perfectly well that he loathed anti-Semitism and German nationalists. He broke with his beloved Nazi sister because of her crackpot opinions—"

"And you think, you *really* think, that the Nazis were completely mistaken when they made a cult of him? All that stuff about 'blond beasts'?"

"Come on, you know better than that. This canard was dead and buried by the time we were in diapers, my friend. When he wrote about blond beasts he didn't mean so-called Aryans, he meant *lions*—majestic beasts. The Nazis lied about Nietzsche as they lied about everything else."

"So Hitler was misguided when he made pilgrimages to the horrible sister in her old age and presented her with flowers?"

"Worse than misguided—sinister. Nietzsche would have been disgusted, but nothing about mindless humanity would have surprised him."

"This is all too easy, my friend. What about his infatuation with cruelty? He always hammers away"—Danny pounds his fist into his palm—"that humanity went into decline when aristocratic superiority was sublimated into pity. He *hammers*. That's his—what do you call it?—his calling card. It's his big idea. Take that away from Nietzsche and he's got nothing, he's naked."

"That's so literal-minded, Danny. Nietzsche's much too subtle and allusive to take off his mask. He's not Sade, he's a pussycat. He's toying with you. He wants to make sure you're worthy of him. When he writes about 'cruelty' or 'violence,' he means forthrightness, strength of character. He leveled about who he was. He knew he harbored the desire to conquer and destroy—sure, what else wasn't new? All the accursed priesthoods of all the God-fearing religions had succeeded in turning humanity's wholesome lust for aggression against ourselves. We grew a self-poisoned apple—guilt. So, to save the world from its misery, Nietzsche told the truth about himself, showed that there was nothing majestic about self-punishment or ressentiment, and sprinkled his work with blood-curdling cries. But there's no evidence he ever so much as swatted a fly. During his military service, he never saw action, though he did injure himself riding an unruly horse."

The mask crinkles. Danny is smiling. "That's very cute, but I'm not convinced."

"I'll bet you think that when he recommends 'philosophizing with a hammer' he means committing intellectual violence, smashing things up. That's a misunderstanding. What he means is tapping the idols, delicately, to find out whether they're solid or hollow, or what. Like a doctor."

"Nietzsche the delicate soul. Alan, you're generous."

"I am when I want to be, yes. You know, just the other day I came across this letter. Where is it? Wait a minute." I scramble through my journal and find the quote: "'I would like to *take away* from human existence some of its heartbreaking and cruel character.'"

Danny gets up and paces around the room as if he's a lion, a caged one. He's excited! That's the important thing.

It means that whatever he says, his metabolism approves of the book.

"Moreover," I toss to the lion, "in my version of Nietzsche, if I want to use my wisdom not to hurt people but to teach them to respect the higher values, if that's where my choices lead, then good for me. Nietzsche doesn't want to produce Nietzsche clones. He wants us to invent values, not copy his."

"I don't know if you really believe this stuff," he says. "Do you?"

"Sit down," I say. "You're making me nervous."

He stops in his tracks and slaps himself mildly on the cheek. "You see, Nietzsche makes *me* nervous." He turns the chair backward and sits down facing me. "OK? So answer my question." I can't read his expression behind the mask.

"I don't know. I don't know. But Nietzsche is right about one fundamental: You matter more than your thought. You should think what makes you feel more alive. And Nietzsche makes me feel more alive."

"So he's the feel-good philosopher?"

That stops me. "That's good, Danny, if you're going to challenge a guy with a needle running into the back of his hand."

"Alan—"

"Don't apologize," I tease him. "It's unseemly. But I take your point. If I were a publisher, I'd stamp the paperback: 'The feel-good philosopher for people who feel bad.'"

Danny lifts his eyebrows—*this* I can see over his mask. "Listen, it's a nice move you make, my friend, turning Nietzsche into the Buddha. I think that what you're saying is that he offers, eh, the consolation prize. He is a consolation thinker, not a breakthrough thinker."

"You put it too strongly, Danny, but that's what interests me."

"No, my dear, I put it too weakly! Nietzsche is a booster for fragile men who believe they will get stronger by saving civilization! Or at least they will torment a society that despises them but needs them whether it knows it or not."

"Friedrich Nietzsche's lonely hearts club band."

"Exactly. I see you are getting healthy. You are holding out for transcendence."

"I am holding out, anyway."

He thinks I have two choices. I can decide that Nietzsche is all of a piece, in which case, if I can't stomach Nietzsche's scorn for democracy and his misogyny (which even during his lifetime outraged his female friends), I have to reconsider the reasons why I find him exemplary in any respect. Or, if Nietzsche is *not* all of a piece, his self-contradictions are so intense as to cast doubt on his coherence altogether.

I tell Danny that it is the self-contradictions that interest me and that if Nietzsche doesn't mind picking cherries, why should I? This is shallow and he says so. I insist that a man on his back in a hospital bed is entitled to a certain shallowness, and if Nietzsche is frivolous, which he may well be, that is all the more interesting. I add that, moreover, I am not trying to resurrect or even vouch for Nietzsche's whole line of thought, but (a) his contradictions are the ones to be fascinated by; (b) it's worth pushing them, seeing how far they'll bend and where the breaking points are; and (c) by whatever bizarre means, and however irregularly, Nietzsche, or my version of Nietzsche, happened upon a whole lot of wisdom about how to live, including the joy of frivolity. Danny says that if I can convince a reader today to care about this wild-eyed German, I will have an interesting book even if I am projecting my own *meshugas* onto a brilliant but crazy seducer who will only let me down hard. I tell him my wife agrees with him. I pump up the back of the hospital bed—this conversation excites me. I am having a splendid time. It would be even better with a bottle of wine between us. Danny grins and pats my cheek.

⌑ ⌑ ⌑

HOME, WITHOUT NAUSEA, despair, or the need for permission to drink a glass of wine. Instead, every morning, when I open my medicine chest, I behold my pharmacopoeia laid out in its plenitude, a double row of white plastic vials. Suggestion to the pharmaceutical industry: Pills should be issued either in little liquor bottles, as in minibars, or in the form of living things with green shoots and tender buds to reveal themselves as what they are—gardens of earthly relief.

I resume the hypodermic ritual. I'm already an old hand at the Neulasta shots in my belly—proceeding around the circumference of a circle whose radius is three inches from my navel, to be technical; finding a spot I haven't poked yet; swabbing with alcohol; pressing the plunger; tossing the finished syringe. I notice that the little scar northwest of my navel, from my biopsy, refuses to fade. I'm managing.

A better word is *maintaining*. That's what Ramón, one of the doormen, always says when you ask him how he's doing. He stretches out the word: main-*tain*-ing. He explains one day that *maintaining* is an all-purpose answer, since if you felt good before and you still feel good, the good feeling is what you're maintaining, and if you don't feel so good, you can think back to another time when you felt not so good, in which case you're maintaining your not-so-good feeling. Either way, you're *maintaining*.

It's a Nietzschean mind game, a cheery one. We're all maintaining, holding our breaths. But in fact, I'm doing more than maintaining. During the hour or two or three when I shake loose of the chemo hangover and also of the texts I have to teach, I continue my push into Nietzsche, leaving behind *Human, All Too Human*, intending to head back into that familiar but still always astonishing territory of *Dawn*, *Joyful Knowledge*, *Beyond Good and Evil*, and *The Genealogy of Morals* as into a jungle redolent of sweet scents and poisonous flowers. . . . But after a few days of reading and rereading the same passages, like a little engine that can't quite make it up the next hill, I have to face the inevitable. My mind's not nearly sharp enough to follow Nietzsche through all his arabesques, whiplash reversals, and catapults to a higher plane (which turns out to be a trampoline)—or I follow him only crudely, from a distance, and myopically, catching the rough silhouettes of his propositions but not the fine grain. This is no way to read a lightning mind. He jokes that he philosophizes with a hammer, but it is more like a jeweler's screwdriver. As long as my mind is blotto, I can't catch his meanings as he really meant them. I should take up a different line of work.

Lemons and lemonade and all that. So I will divert myself with the minor biographies, including, for fun, Lou Salomé's, published in 1894, when he was still alive. My German's rusty, but I'm not in an awful hurry.

So, in Nietzschean fashion, my days overflow. It's a paradoxical condition: I am lounging under the sword, yet I have all the time in the world. If I finish, I finish; if not, not.

⌑ ⌑ ⌑

I WONDER HOW Garry McGinnis is doing, and with whom. I could probably find out if I chose to.

⌑ ⌑ ⌑

February 20

For some reason, today's look in the mirror horrifies me. I look haunted—or rather, I look like the haunter. My eyes accuse—whom? Sad and bewildered, they stare out as if from the bottom of a deep hole. My face is so gaunt I might just as well have stepped out of solitary confinement. *See what you've done to me!*

Then I'm amused—make that almost amused. I'm *fashionably* gaunt, metrosexually so. Sir Alan of Gaunt. My face has re-formed around sculpted cheekbones. I could model chemotherapy outfits.

¤ ¤ ¤

February 21

A cab with Melanie back to Sloan-Kettering for my final round of chemotherapy. By now, I'm a pro. Still, on the way across bone-white Central Park, holding Melanie's hand, I have little flashes of the *why me?* whine that I thought I'd got free of. This time, for the two-night stay, I've brought along Lou Salomé as well as Henning Mankell's *The White Lioness*. Dear Julia, my old friend, sent me a shipment of thrillers; the Mankell was the most literate of them. I looked through *Lioness* last night and it was perfect: Its sinister mood matches mine. A few years ago, when I picked up one of Mankell's Swedish police novels, something grotesque happened in the opening pages, something so grisly I repressed the exact memory. I shut the book and decided to leave him alone. Now life has toughened me.

¤¤¤

THE CLICK-CLACK OF stiletto heels on the other side of the door of Dr. Berg's examining room. Enter Dr. Berg, plucky and chipper. She notes the Salomé cover photo of "the holy trinity"—the author in the cart not quite convincingly holding her whip on Nietzsche and Paul Rée.

"Nietzsche," she says. "Wasn't he kind of a Nazi?"

"It's a calumny," I say, "except coming from his sister, for whom it was a compliment."

"Well, enjoy."

My white count has recovered, and I'm ready for round three. I fish for a prognosis. Results for the protocol remain "stellar," she says. I ask for a reminder why I'm classified as "high-intermediate risk." She reminds me that the original scans showed evidence, if only slightly, that the disease, which was mostly on the downtown end of my torso, had also spread above my diaphragm.

With this, I feel a mental shudder, a tremor. It's as if a melodramatic horror-movie organ sounds a protracted chord. *I have cancer.* Have? Had? Once more the bottom falls out and I plunge into a pit. There are questions best left unasked, as Nietzsche should have taught me. This is why I prefer him to Socrates. But I still haven't driven the fussy little Athenian out of my system. The need to *know*, to strain to *know more*, to catch a glimpse of what lies around the bend—face it, this is a faith in magic. We want oracles, not doctors.

By the time I check in to the admitting desk, I'm in a blur. I've gone unreal. Melanie's gone unreal. Even Dr. Berg is unreal except for the old news about how far the disease had progressed before it was "melted away." I didn't feel like living quite this dangerously, thank you, Dr. Nietzsche.

Waiting room for admitting: a goofy comedy on the TV, a pair of loud headphones leaking the sounds of Ella Fitzgerald singing "Love Is Here to Stay." A nurse takes me into an examining room.

"Any restrictions on your arm?"

"Excuse me?"

She repeats, a little slower, as if I'm slow, which I probably am.

"No, no, I'm always ready." She jabs the needle in and a tremendous pain, a kind of electric jolt, slashes through the back of my hand and up my arm to my shoulder. I feel a little eruption of flaming anger that I have to be subjected to this. I'm a caged, tortured baboon.

Because I *had* cancer. *Had*. Can we just be done with the anticlimax, people, once and for all, can we just fucking be done?

"Why do you have to stick me in the back of my hand?"

"It's most convenient."

For you. But you mean no harm, and some pain I can overlook.

¤¤¤

GOETHE COMPLAINED ABOUT poets who wrote "as if they were ill and the whole world a hospital." Little did he know how far things would go. He'd never met a New York intellectual. He had the luxury of not having an IV line run into the back of his hand during his span on earth.

So here I am, back in a hospital bed in time for lunch, rigged again by a lifeline to a mobile pole. There's a leaden sky, the usual menu, and no TV noise. I haven't given up expecting Garry McGinnis to slouch in and clarify the intrigue of his life. But there's no Garry McGinnis, or anyone else. Actually, I'm relieved. Silence is freedom, is warmth, is balm. For company, once Melanie leaves, there's only Lou Salomé and Henning Mankell. But they should be enough.

When Salomé published the original, Nietzsche was still alive, though gravely demented. Lady Lou has the authority of a former lover—someone who sees your faults even more clearly than she sees your strengths, but whose testimony is buttressed on both sides.

The moment when you open a book is always a moment of truth, like a first date, with feints, aromas, hints of seduction or error or farce in the air. Soon enough I am rewarded. On the fourth page of her first section, "Nietzsche's Essence,"

Lou announces her theme, quoting from a Nietzsche letter of 1879 to Paul Rée: "I've avoided death's door several times, but was terribly tortured—and so, I live from day to day, and each day tells a story of sickness." To have Lou Salomé smile upon my project—a woman who smiled upon Nietzsche in the flesh, and was smiled upon by him—gives me goose bumps.

Her writing is gummy. But she can write with a hammer when she wants to. After a few aimless pages she gets hold of her theme and pounds it. She is setting out to link his agonies to his thinking! A few pages on, she notes his "individual aphorisms, strewn throughout his works, about the *value of suffering for the gain of knowledge*." Her italics.

I read on, hardly breathing, as Frau Lou continues: Each time Nietzsche "declines into sickness," he lunges forward, for "every recuperation becomes his own rebirth and with it all of life around him—and as always, the pain is 'entwined in the victory.'" Nietzsche's "almost rhythmic up and down of mental conditions . . . , in the final analysis, seems to stem from nothing else than *falling ill because of* thoughts and recuperating through thoughts." Her italics again.

She waters her insight and it buds into a theory. Nietzsche has an "urge for self-laceration" because *he needs it* to renew his thinking! Suffering is his madeleine. It permits him to digest what he has already understood and opens him up to what he is going to understand next. Thus the herky-jerky movement of his somersaults and leaps. There comes an electric moment when he is seized and refreshed by a new insight, he feels the thrill of it entering into him, but the very next moment "he is immediately gripped again by something like a fever or restlessly surging overflow of inner energy that ultimately turns its sting against him: he is the cause of his self-induced illness." This half-sentence she doesn't italicize, so I will: *He is the cause of his self-induced illness.*

As I thought, illness is the key to Nietzsche's passion for strength. I feel vindicated, oddly elated. And doze.

I'm awakened by an electronic alarm blaring behind me. A nurse enters—there's a kink in the line, and the elixir is not flowing. She unkinks the line, then smiles beneficently. The alarm stops. I recall my pleasure that the intensely perceptive Lou Salomé—mistress to, or collaborator in, an entire civilization (Nietzsche! Freud! Rilke!)—is on my side.

This is enough experience for one day. I read myself to sleep with the serviceable Mankell.

¤ ¤ ¤

February 23

If my luck holds, this is my last morning at Sloan-Kettering, a territory bounded by hope, faith, and doggedness. And fear.

After breakfast and the *Times*, I walk my pole over to the chair at the window (the sky still leaden, the river still gleaming, the bridge still traffic-choked) and dive back into Lou Salomé. For pages on end she slides back into her viscous style, a clunky sentimentality of longings and urges, at least in translation, but I am more and more impressed by her psychological acumen, which is less jagged than Nietzsche's own, less brilliant, less supple, and far less pungent—but I can see why Nietzsche thought she was qualified to be his disciple, though she declined the privilege. For example, she notes the paradox that Nietzsche's "battle against rapture and his glorification of the unemotional appear simply as attempts at inducing rapture by ravaging himself." Delicious. The counterposition of "rapture" and "ravage" in English is a felicitous touch.

Lou Salomé saw through the conventional dismissal of Nietzsche as a will-freak who was so frightened of women that he "often" (as he wrote just days after the Trampedach episode) struggled to "escape accusing himself of unmanliness." Lou could look unflinchingly but with eye-rolling amusement at the grotesque misogyny that led him to write garbage like this:

> One-half of mankind is weak, chronically sick, changeable, inconstant. . . . [S]he needs a religion of weakness that glorifies being weak, love and humility as divine: or better still, she makes the strong weak—she succeeds in overcoming the strong. Woman has always conspired with decadent types—the priests, for instance—against the "mighty," the "strong," the men.

Lou understood that women didn't need to be lectured about living on the slopes of Vesuvius. She saw this nonsense for what it was, a pathetic quirk. She knew that the heart of Nietzsche's system of thought was his confrontation with illness, his attempt to use it, to live with it, and—with the knife of his mind—to slice through it. She grasped that his aphoristic method was "forced upon Nietzsche by his illness and the way he lived." The vitality that he lionized, the health that was the greatest gift that human life could deliver—it was, just as I thought, the health of a sick man. Frau Lou had this insight more than a century ago.

But slow down, Alan. Hold on. Think this through. Lou doesn't *exactly* agree with you—or with Nietzsche. She gives priority *to his mind*. She maintains that first, he thinks himself sick, and second, his sickness spurs him to think new thoughts. Her line of reasoning is precisely the opposite of Nietzsche's "Start from the body"! Lou is his *overenthusiastic* disciple, affirming the will to power as if the will *rules* the body outright, as if it is omnipotent—the power of Nietzsche's mind to take the whip to his body. She has turned Nietzsche into a psychosomatic masochist.

But this is also exactly the sort of neat, pat, assured, X-causes-Y argument that Nietzsche normally scorns.

Lou's mind is ferocious. No wonder she had the whip hand in the photo.

¤ ¤ ¤

When Melanie arrives to take me home, I'm woozy from decrepitude and disuse. She helps me get dressed. She has her hand at my elbow so I can rise to my feet.

Home, after two nights away, is the zone of relief that it was before, that it always was, orderly and cushioned, clean and well lighted. Natasha is out. Home is the place where, when you've been discharged from the hospital, they have to take you in. I'm ready to be here.

And celebrate by taking a nap.

I wake up an hour and a half later, almost refreshed.

I don't want to sink back into a life caged in my bedroom, so after washing up, I take Lou's book—we're on a first-name basis now—into the living room. After opening the cover, I close it again. Enough for the moment—I lay her book aside, pick up a volume of Nietzsche's letters, lie down on the couch.

Melanie comes over with a tall glass of water, hands it to me, reminds me to keep drinking as per hospital instructions, since it's time to wash the poisons away now that they've done their work. "Come sit down," I say. I hunch back against the cushions, she sits down abutting my hip bone, peers at the Salomé book on the end table, then at the book lying upside down on my chest.

"Him again," she says.

"Him again."

We bathe in a silence of love and relief.

"I'm glad you're home."

We touch lips with the sure lightness of long acquaintance and the paradoxical promise of pleasant surprise.

"I'm not so sure I feel that way about *him*," she says. "The house madman."

⌑ ⌑ ⌑

A COUPLE OF days pass. I take pills and give myself shots in the belly. I feel no nausea. I sleep. I taste the sweetness of sweet potatoes, the pep of pepper. From the corner of the living room, I gaze at the northernmost edge of the saffron-colored cloth "gates" that the court provocateurs who call themselves Christo and Jeanne-Claude installed in Central Park—these hokey picture-postcard illuminations that promise everything gorgeous and provisional, and nothing at all. I am at home.

I think about Nietzsche's faith that the will to power is the heart of life. I think of him leaving one ferocious and exquisite reminder after another—to himself and anyone else audacious enough to face the wholeness of life that he is willing to face—that there is a heartbeat in the mind. I know I need the maximum of my will to vitality—what the grand provocateur calls the will to power—to keep me humming along in the belief that I'll pull through. My own will to power demands that I tangle myself in hope and fear for my daughter, and still pull through.

Nietzsche's plunge into the depths and masks of his own life is *his* plunge. What he wants is that we take plunges of our own.

As the days pass, Natasha plunges inexorably into a life that will be like nothing she has imagined.

"So," I say while she's washing the dishes.

"So?"

"Steady as she goes?"

"Fine. Honestly. All is well."

"And if I ask about the mysterious father—"

"Dad, here's something you have to understand. It was a one-night stand. He's so over. It's finished. OK?"

¤¤¤

"THERE WERE DAYS when we never thought we'd be lying in bed, just—lying here," I say to Melanie. We stare at the ceiling from two separate pillows. "But I just feel like lying."

"You'll be back." She leans over and kisses me on the cheek. It's poignant, as in the sharp point of a sword—and sometimes more than poignant—to recall our long-lost days of erotic delirium, the always surprising delight in the discovery of how *this* feels and how *that* feels, of acute anticipation of what our bodies might have in store for us next time. Always, *always*, those days were succeeded by spells of melancholia. The delirium weakened us, and we stumbled out into the world depleted.

"Your job is to recover from cancer. Don't worry."

"How are *you*?" I ask eventually.

"It's been hard."

"You've been wonderful, darling. I haven't said that enough. Wonderful." I blink hard. There's a reservoir of gratitude behind my eyes.

"You know, about Natasha, I only think of the future. About you, I only think of the present."

That seems about right to me.

"And now that you're home, sweetheart," she goes on, "there's something I have to tell you."

"You're sick and tired of me and cancer, and you've fallen in love with a dashing young—"

She makes a sour face. "I'm going to overlook that ridiculous remark."

"I'm sorry, but darling, you never have to stand in line to say something to me."

She flicks her index finger at the cover photo on the Salomé volume lying next to the bed. "That's us, the unholy triangle."

"Ha, ha."

"I guess I'm cast as the one with the whip. Not very realistic. But sweetheart, sweetheart, really, here you are just out of the hospital and you're immersed in him, not just one Nietzsche book but two of them"—pointing at the book of letters—"and what I want you to think about is, just think about it, OK, you don't have to say anything now, I know it's great that you never stopped working during all this and now you're roaring right back into work, but really, is it such a terrific idea to spend so much time going on about Nietzsche the sick man?"

"You mean, as opposed to—"

"I mean, as opposed to, I don't know, you'll think of something. . . ."

She trails off.

"The sunnier side of life? Hallmark Nation?"

"Stop putting words in my mouth! I don't mean a smiley—"

"Nobody ever accused me—"

"Excuse me! I was talking!"

"Sorry. Sorry!"

She glares.

"Please go on."

Having proved that I'm a boor, she goes on. "OK, so first of all, Nietzsche's an old story."

"But—"

"Hold on. He's *your* old story. Second, *he was a crazy person.*"

"Hold on yourself. He *went* crazy, that's certainly true, but before that, we should all be crazy like that—"

"That's what scares me! You think that. It's bad enough that we have to live with George Bush—"

"Well, as a matter of fact, Bush isn't irrelevant to this. Writing about Nietzsche purges me. It keeps me, I don't know, slightly constructive."

"I know you think that. I'm not so sure."

"Well, we'll find out. I'm performing the experiment. As for how long he was going crazy, we'll never know. He *went* crazy, there's no doubt about that, his views of women were *meshugeh*, strutting, kindergarten-level misogynist stuff, that's true too, but until 1888 his style is brilliant, not crazy, or let me put it this way, it's brilliant despite crazy, or—" I make air-quotes—"'crazy,' and not brilliant *because* crazy. He's wild, he's raw, he's primitive. He takes flying leaps. The question is what's the relation between his wildness and this line of thought he produced, which was so influential and, if you don't mind, important—"

"Excuse me! Darling, I say this to you with all love and respect, but you have a passion for crazy. You love it. You *admire* it. You think it's grand and exalted. I liked it too when I was twenty-one. Isn't it time to get over it?"

"You're telling me I should grow up."

"I'm telling you that you've been through an ordeal and you need to be healthy, *I* need you to be healthy, and I don't think this obsession is good for you, and Nietzsche believes in overcoming yourself, so overcome yourself!"

I recognize a strong move, but I'm not done yet. "Have you considered that I might insulate myself from illness by writing about it? On the inoculation principle?"

"You know what I think? I think you're a reactionary. You react. I say *up*, you say *down*. Which is why I was reluctant to say any of this before."

"But you thought it."

"Of course I thought it. How could I not think it?"

This conversation has gone as far as it can go.

"Just promise me," she says, "that you'll think about what I'm saying."

"I'll think about it."

"Up!"

"Up!"

We exchange high-fives.

¤ ¤ ¤

MARCH BLOWS IN, along with some crazy happiness. My white blood count goes up. The saffron "gates" come down. I like to think that I'm recovering my life, or a semblance of it. I'm still weak and mentally blurred, but I feel *protected*. Melanie works away on an overdue manuscript, looking for all the world as if she did not just usher her husband through cancer, though God knows what scars she's carrying around inside. I don't know, and don't want to prod her, which would only remind her of her ordeal.

She starts letting me walk to class on my own. I'm disappointed that she stops attending. I had thought it was my brilliance and, of course, the intrinsic merits of the subject matter, not her solicitude, that had led her to accompany me. It turns out that she was only afraid that I'd walk into traffic. Natasha bounds around the apartment, lithe and less hangdog than before. Friends drop by and lie that I look good. I inject Neulasta into my belly like a pro. I drink wine. My libido revives—quivers, at any rate.

In this state of recovery I go on reading about Nietzsche. The signs are everywhere that he knows exactly what he's doing—saving himself by thinking. Here is a letter of April 10, 1888, in which he thinks back to that awful time when he was deciding to walk away from his professorship in Basel: "My specialty was to endure the extremity of pain, *cru*, *vert*, with complete lucidity for two or three days in succession, with continuous vomiting of mucus. . . . *During this terrible period my mind even attained maturity.*" The thought grows on me that, with his acute self-knowledge, he must be deeply aware that his system of self-overcoming is a therapeutic exercise. A mind game. A mental ploy for making the most of his sickliness.

I pick up *Conversations with Nietzsche*. Ida Overbeck, the perceptive wife of his trusted friend Franz, says: "He hoped to regain his health by his way of thinking." He *hoped*. But his thinking fell short, and he knew it. He wanted a God who knew how to dance, but he was not that God himself. At least in private moments, he knew it. A man named Sebastian Hausmann, who met Nietzsche during a walk in the mountains, recalled "that he occasionally fell into strange contradictions. When on one occasion I took the liberty to call such a contradiction to his attention, I noticed very clearly that this made him nervous, so I did not do it again." Maybe this Hausmann put Nietzsche off. Maybe Nietzsche appeared nervous because, always sensitive and impressionable, he reflected back Hausmann's own nervousness. A lot of maybes. That's the point: You don't know.

There are disconcerting surprises—which is exciting if you're a straight biographer with an open mind but somewhat offputting if you're a philosopher theorizing about the fit between the life and his work and you may have the life wrong. There's testimony that Nietzsche didn't avoid small talk at all: "Nietzsche never despised the simple things that came across his path." There's testimony that, despite his headaches and horrible vision, he *did* read—profusely, by one account. So what if, on some small points but also on some not so small, I've been working with dubious facts? I fancy that I've been getting to know him well enough to theorize, but what if I'm kidding myself? What if, amid all the information I'm relying on, the ratio of misinformation to solid information is so high that my whole jury-rigged idea is shaky? It's hard enough to write your own story, let alone a dead man's.

This is the goddamned thing about biography, even autobiography, even quasi-biography, as opposed to straightforward, down-home, text-based, interpretive philosophy. You're tightly bound to awkward old facts. Facts may be elusive and subject to interpretation, but in the end, they're tough little bastards, and they can crack your teeth when you bite down on them clumsily, throw your nifty interpretation way out of whack. So what if the syphilis theory of his state of mind is right, that he started to develop symptoms when he was in his twenties, that his whole wild system of thought is a fever chart? How much is known anyway about the exact sequence in which syphilitic symptoms appear? Am I going to conduct a medical inquest?

And then suppose I actually get to the point where I know the facts about Nietzsche's existence on earth superlatively—and suppose that I arrive at an ironclad thesis about the relation between his life and his work, namely, the hookup of the illness-in-body and health-in-theory themes—wouldn't it be worse than wrong? Wouldn't it be awfully pat? Wouldn't it chop off everything paradoxical, "everything lush, colorful, blossoming, illusory, everything that charms and is alive" about Nietzsche? I'm sick and tired of pat. I conclude my conclusions.

Face it. This book I've been living for is worse than an overreach: It's a dead end. And even if it weren't an overreach, how would I keep it from reading like a *Reader's Digest* inspirational tale?

Then maybe I'm left with the literary equivalent of the journalism of failure, like Gay Talese's chronicle of his failure to interview Frank Sinatra. Or the cinema vérité of failure, like that documentary by the Australian guy who tried to interview Fidel Castro, and failed, and failed, and finally made a movie called *Waiting for Fidel*, which was the story of his failures. There's a lot of this around these days. I can see it coming: *The Nietzsche Folly*; or, *The Presumption of an Ignorant Man*; or, *How, in the Spirit of Nietzsche, I Danced Away.*

¤¤¤

BUT DID I write those words? *This book I've been living for*?

What an absurd thing to say. Worse than absurd: spiteful, pathetic. An insult to my wife, my child, my friends, and all the colors of life. An insult to the living, animal health that I've been telling myself I live for. I would seem to have learned nothing from Nietzsche.

Part of me must believe in the archaic, absurd, presumptuous fantasy that I've been living to write a book—a book that, unlike Nietzsche's, will not change the world.

¤¤¤

SELF-PITY IS THE cry of the wounded animal. But the wound itself cries out in a robust voice: *I am.*

¤¤¤

WHAT IS THE wound, anyway? My hair is growing back—finer and softer than before, but it covers the same terrain, leaving the same bald dome. It's no more white than before. It's *my hair.*

I'm not going to live forever. I know it now. Not that, before, I thought that I was going to live forever. So what's changed?

Now I'll make a home in my mortality. It's *my mortality*. Mine.

¤ ¤ ¤

IT OCCURS TO me that now, with the chemo finished, I'm unprotected. Naked.

This thought comes with a chill, and a ripple of something I can only call joy.

¤ ¤ ¤

I LOOK OUT the window. Fleets of yellow cabs are rolling down Broadway. A man in baggy jeans, younger than I, lugs a huge sack of empty plastic water bottles, hundreds of them, along the sidewalk and stops to poke through a waste basket in search of more. A police car passes two men waiting to cross the street, and the driver, he or she, shoots them a little squirt of the siren—a brush back, to remind them who owns the street. Never mind, other pedestrians pausing on other traffic islands will go on stepping out from their curbs, testing the traffic for irresoluteness. Millions of mortals are denying, racing, zigzagging, schlepping, moping, exulting, bullying, cutting their swaths through the city, every one of them mortal. I think they're fools, most of them, and I'm content that they should think the same of me.

Absurd to be at war with them, to be cruel to them, to feel bitter, or spiteful, or exempt, or to aspire to save them, or to demand that the world make sense.

¤ ¤ ¤

March 25

I drink the banana-flavored potion, and an attendant slides me back into the narrow torus of the CAT scan, for what is to be the first in a series, every four months for some number of years. *Breathe in. . . . Hold your breath. . . . Breathe.* In the last stage, my body goes warm. I hope this is a good sign.

¤ ¤ ¤

March 28

Somehow Dr. Berg's waiting room succeeds in not looking gloomy. Fluorescence dispels shadows. There's an elderly woman knitting. The impressionist posters are pretty good, if derivative. But none of this is the reason, exactly.

The click-clack of her heels up to the door; two light, quick knocks; and she comes in clutching the CAT scan report.

"It's great," she says cheerily.

I tell her I have begun to feel exposed now, anxious, because I'm no longer being shot up with chemo.

"A lot of people feel that way," she says.

But they did melt the blob away, as promised.

⌑ ⌑ ⌑

April—May—I set aside hours to go over the medical bills that flow in, imprinted with more and more imperious messages. I write checks. I appeal. I have extended conversations with the hospital finance office and the insurance company. I appeal denials of my appeals. I wonder how people manage all this if they don't have insurance, or time, or a degree in mathematics or a PhD.

⌑ ⌑ ⌑

June 15

I go to the dentist. He asks me routinely how I've been. *Not well, actually.* Oh? *I had lymphoma.* I like the sound of the past tense. I *had* it. I was treated. I tell him I have to get scanned every four months now. He listens, then says,

"So you're in remission."

Well, if you want to put it that way, I want to say, but don't. I would prefer to say, *It's gone.* I had it, like: I had a cold.

Re-mis-sion. *n.* 1. a lessening of the symptoms of a disease, or their temporary reduction or disappearance.

I prefer the word *reprieve*. Re-prieve. n. 1. the halting or delay of somebody's punishment, especially when the punishment is death. It's awfully romantic.

¤ ¤ ¤

July 15

PET scan followed by CAT scan. The usual indignities, the usual faux banana concoction, the usual pain in the back of my hand as the needle is jammed in, the usual metallic taste in the mouth, the usual incongruity of being inserted into a machine. The usual suspense.

¤ ¤ ¤

July 18

Dr. Berg: "If I was a betting person, I would sell you life insurance. I think you're going to do beautifully."

The results from the Sloan-Kettering protocol so far are "terrific." She waves a graph in front of me, something about EFSes. "What's an EFS?" I ask. Event-free survival. So far, of the more than a hundred patients enrolled, it looks as though there's been only one recurrence, and no deaths. I don't study the chart very carefully, or ask any more questions.

⌑⌑⌑

NATASHA SWELLS. HER jawline is more rounded. Her skin takes on that translucent look of women in Renaissance paintings.

⌑⌑⌑

MELANIE SAYS TO me one day: "You've disappeared into yourself. You're not there."

I tell her that *she's* the one who's retreated, or maybe the whole world has. But she's telling the truth.

"I'm masking my feelings," I say. "Nietzsche, you know, says, 'Everything deep loves masks.'"

"Nietzsche *is* your mask."

⌑⌑⌑

THEY *DID* MELT the tumor away. Not myself.

⌑⌑⌑

ON THE DAY I decide I will publish this journal, I go for a walk in Riverside Park.

The air is screaming with spring. The green is the most vivid possible green. If there were a planet where for some chemical reason chlorophyll were red, that red could not be a brighter red than the foliage here is stunningly green.

A security guard taking a break sits on a bench contemplating his belly. I think that he is at peace with it and with his own scars.

A couple of blocks down, a young couple stand on the sidewalk, kissing. Next to them stands a baby carriage. I pass them, walk another few blocks, turn back. The couple have not changed position. They are still kissing.

This happened. It is not a cheap romantic image. Perhaps it's an expensive one.

I am not one to disdain sentimentality.

¤ ¤ ¤

THE LITTLE SCAR northwest of my navel remains—refusing, like me, to vanish.

To Hudson Kidwell, born August 3, 2005

¤ ¤ ¤

Acknowledgments

All quotations and most biographical elements derive from Nietzsche's published works as well as Curtis Cate, *Friedrich Nietzsche* (New York: Overlook Press, 2005); Curt Paul Janz, *Friedrich Nietzsche, Biographie*, Erster Band (München/Wien: Carl Hanser Verlag, 1978); Christopher Middleton, ed. and trans., *Selected Letters of Friedrich Nietzsche* (Chicago: University of Chicago Press, 1969); Peter Fuss and Henry Shapiro, eds. and trans., *Nietzsche: A Self-Portrait from His Letters* (Cambridge, MA: Harvard University Press, 1971); Sander L. Gilman, ed., *Conversations with Nietzsche: A Life in the Words of His Contemporaries*, trans. David J. Parent (New York: Oxford University Press, 1987); Lou Salomé, *Nietzsche*, trans. Siegfried Mandel (Champaign: University of Illinois Press, 2001, first published 1894); and Pierre Klossowski, *Nietzsche and the*

Vicious Circle, trans. Daniel W. Smith (Chicago: University of Chicago Press, 1997).

Translations are by Siegfried Mandel, Dalya Bilu, Walter Kauffmann, Peter Fuss and Henry Shapiro, Christopher Middleton, and Daniel W. Smith, sometimes modified by the author.

For an education in Nietzsche, I am indebted to John Richardson. For reading drafts and working them over with hammers, I am indebted to Liel Leibovitz, Elizabeth Harlan, Laurel Cook, Marshall Berman, and the late Jack Diggins.